OPEN ROADS, OPEN HEARTS

A TRAVELLER'S JOURNEY

RUFINA AJALIE

Open Roads, Open Hearts: A Traveller's Journey

Copyright © 2025 by Rufina Ajalie

Paperback ISBN: 978-1-963732-29-0
Hardback ISBN: 978-1-963732-30-6

Published by
The Publishing Pad
www.thepublishingpad.com

Table of Contents

A Note to the Reader v

Prologue. 1

Chapter One A Rainy Night in Rome. 5

Chapter Two Sanctuary 13

Chapter Three Choices 19

Chapter Four The Jump 25

Chapter Five Not Bound. 29

Chapter Six The Page Turner 33

Chapter Seven Setting Out. 37

Chapter Eight The Tuscan Way 41

Chapter Nine The Return to Rome. 47

Chapter Ten The City Wants to Know the Truth 53

Chapter Eleven The Quiet That Comes Between Pages 61

Chapter Twelve The Old Rough Road 69

Chapter Thirteen Finding My Voice. 79

Chapter Fourteen A Surprise Love in Marrakech. 85

Chapter Fifteen Florence 93

Chapter Sixteenth The Shadow and the Light 99

Chapter Seventeen The Legacy of Love 105

Chapter Eighteen The Return of the Sun 109

Chapter Nineteen A Letter to the Future 113

Chapter Twenty The Interval Between 117

Chapter Twenty-One The Turning Light 125

Epilogue Open Roads, Open Hearts 129

Author's Note 133

About the Author. 137

A Note to the Reader

After years of losing pieces of herself to work, marriage, and the quiet expectations of others, Sophia wakes one morning in Rome with nothing left but exhaustion. Until a quiet encounter in a small bookstore offers her something she hasn't felt in years: stillness.

This is the story of her return to herself, through volunteer work, unexpected friendships, quiet moments in unfamiliar cities, and a soft, slow-blooming connection with a man who sees her clearly but asks for nothing in return.

From the crowded streets of Rome to the cliffs of Sicily and the peaceful fields of Tuscany, Sophia learns how to breathe again. How to choose again. How to come home to the woman she lost along the way.

If you have ever felt stuck, unseen, or afraid to begin again, I hope this story reminds you that it is never too late to start listening to yourself.

Prologue

I was lost, not in the winding aisles of a Roman bookstore but in the quiet, dark corners of my own life. It is the kind of loss that comes slowly, like a shadow moving across a room when you aren't looking. It settles into the soft spots of your routine, like the tired smile you give your coworkers or the polite answers you give to people who aren't really listening.

You wake up one day and realize that you haven't really lived your days. You don't remember the last time you felt something real. You forget that you used to be someone who had an imagination, a hunger, and a pulse.

I used to love how old books smelled. The smell that day only made me think of all the things I had put off: the dreams I had forgotten, the life I had made smaller to get by. I touched the spines with my fingers, as if one of them might lead me back. None of them did. They just sat there, quiet and patient, like old friends when they know you don't want to talk.

I was in my mid-forties, standing at a crossroads I didn't remember choosing. There was a life behind me that was built on smart choices and unfulfilled wants. There was an empty space in front of me that needed someone braver than me.

For almost twenty years, I went through my days as if they belonged to someone else. I wore responsibility like other people wear jewellery. I never thought about putting the weight down. Not until small, quiet things started to break inside me.

Then I met Giovanni.

He shouldn't have been there. Most of the time, the store closed early on rainy nights, and most owners didn't stay after the last customer left. Later, he told me that a late delivery had kept him there, and he had stayed to finish cleaning the counter while the radio played in the background. I didn't plan to stop. He didn't plan to wait. But somehow, we ended up in the same quiet moment, two strangers drawn into a place neither of us meant to be.

He asked what I thought of *Jane Eyre,* the kind of question that comes from someone who actually wants to know. He smiled as if he already knew how it would end, but wanted me to discover it for myself.

We started our conversations with small things. Books. The best gelato ever. How Rome smelled after it rained. He laughed softly and said something about how the sounds of the city are like how Romans talk with the voices, and how the streets seem to carry conversations from one corner to the next. It wasn't noise like people from outside think of it. It was life. A rhythm. A beat. The kind of movement that makes you feel less alone, even when you're by yourself.

He could turn basic ideas into mirrors. I listened more closely than I thought I would, not just to him but also to the city I had lived in for years without really seeing it.

He asked me, "Why do you stay with what feels safe?" one afternoon while we were sitting on a bench near Campo de' Fiori.

His words hit a soft spot. I couldn't look at him.

I said, "Because safe doesn't hurt," but I could feel how empty it was even as I said it.

He didn't tell me I was wrong. He just stood there and watched the square, as if he knew that truth comes out slowly.

That day, something changed inside of me. Not an explosion. A break. There is just enough room for a little light to get in.

Cracks get bigger. And soon, everything I thought I knew about myself started to change.

That chance meeting in a quiet Roman bookstore started a story I never thought would happen. A story about love and loss and about learning how to breathe again after years of not talking.

Now that I look back, I see that this was the time when my life started to get better. The moment I stopped quietly drowning and reached for something more. Not sure. Not perfect. Just take a breath. A chance.

This is the story of how I started to live. My name is Sophia.

CHAPTER ONE

A Rainy Night in Rome

It started to rain right after eight. I turned off my computer and watched the office floor empty one light at a time. The chairs rolled back. The doors of the elevator closed. The last printer coughed and then stopped. I was still there, pretending to finish something important to avoid the silence that awaited me at home.

Via Cavour breathed in the storm outside. Cars hissed as they drove through the wet streets. A motorcycle went by with a blue poncho that looked like a flag. The air smelled like wet stone, exhaust, and coffee that had been sitting out for too long. I pulled my coat tighter and started to walk.

I've lived in Rome long enough to know where to go without thinking. Long enough to know the streets by heart, yet still be surprised by them in small, quiet ways. It had been almost four years since I turned forty, the year when everything in my life changed at once. I was forty-four now, old enough to know better, but still young enough to feel lost in ways that caught me off guard. That year was over, but its weight remained. Time had kept moving, but something in me had stayed behind. I was still trying to understand who I had become after it. It had been long enough that I'd forgotten to look up.

The city is still beautiful even when you don't deserve it. At night, fountains light up. Voices drift out of trattorias and into the dark like songs that don't have to hurry. Rome has conversations in the open air, like some places have wind. It's not noise, like people think it is. It's a heartbeat, a reminder that you're not the only story going on.

I walked past everything. I didn't want to go home yet. I didn't want to answer the same questions that were always there for me. *Are you happy? Is this real life? How much longer will you keep acting?*

I turned down a narrow side street to avoid a crowd and saw a pool of warm light in front of me. An old iron sign with paint on it swung. *Libri e Caffè*. I could hear cups softly clicking and a radio playing softly. The door was still slightly ajar. I pushed it open.

First, I felt warmth. And then the smell. A little bit of lemon peel, sugar, and old paper. There were shelves on one wall from floor to ceiling. There were novels in two languages next to each other. The wooden floor politely groaned under my feet. A man at the counter looked up. He was holding a cloth in one hand and a cup in the other. His smile didn't ask me to do anything. "Is it open?" I asked.

He said, "For a little while. Rain brings readers who like to think." He put the espresso down too quickly, and a drop of coffee spilled onto the saucer. He didn't seem to care or notice. He wiped his hands on the old apron. He didn't hurry me. There were two students at a table in the back and a woman by the window who closed her book and left a coin for the coffee. As she left, the bell over the door made a soft, thankful sound. With a steady hand, the man behind the counter poured coffee and put the cup on a saucer.

"Please," he said, extending the cup of coffee to me.

I didn't remember telling him what I wanted, but I had. I'd ordered it without thinking. It had a strong, dark flavour and a little heat in the throat. I sat by the window and watched the rain make silver lines on the glass. The edges of the city outside looked softer. I could hear my breathing. I could feel my shoulders begin to drop.

There were times when rainy nights in Rome made me think of Lagos evenings after a long day. The sky would look like it was going to storm, but it would hold off just long enough for the city to keep buzzing. Even tiredness had a rhythm in Lagos. Streetlights flickered over danfo buses full of tired people, hawkers shouted prices for gala and pure water between cars, and someone, somewhere, was always laughing so loudly that people turned to look. It was messy, imperfect, and full of life. It shaped my pulse before I knew what silence was like, even though I didn't always feel like I belonged to it. I realized how long it had been since a place made me feel anything other than numb while I sat here with the rain hitting the window and my breath slowly getting steadier.

He cleaned one table, then another, and then he went back to the counter. No need to rush. Not showing up. His voice was quiet when he spoke, as if we were already in a conversation that didn't need to be pushed.

He said, "You work close by."

"Yes."

"Late at night."

"Too many of them."

He smiled without pity. "I stay up late, too. The peace and quiet help. Not as much noise."

"More truth."

I let the words hang out between us. Truth. It sounded deep and heavy. To keep from staring at him too long, I looked at the shelves. A thin copy of *Jane Eyre* was propped up against a thick book of poems. The corner of the cover of a children's book with a pirate on it was torn, making it look like the pirate was winking. The details made me feel better than I thought they would.

"What is this place?" I asked. "Is it a coffee shop with books or a bookshop with coffee?"

Before he answered, he adjusted his wire-rimmed glasses, a nervous habit, I would come to realize. "It's easier on the eyes," he said. "And it keeps the electricity bill honest, you know?"

He smiled a little, almost shyly. Then he added softly, "But yes, a room where people can breathe and don't feel invisible is important, too."

He wiped his hand on the cloth and set it aside.

"I am Giovanni."

"Sophia."

He said my name again, as if he wanted to make sure he had heard it right. Then he nodded once, as if it was supposed to be there.

After that, we didn't talk much. I drank all of my coffee. He flipped the sign on the door to "Closed," but he didn't touch the lock. The students hurriedly packed their bags and left, talking quietly about a test. The room's rhythm slowed down. I saw that someone had used clear glue to seal a crack in the window frame. A postcard of the Tuscan hills was hidden behind the register. A small jar of sugar with a spoon that had lost its shine. There was nothing special about it. It was all of it.

"Do you read?" he said, looking at the cups he was drying.

"I used to," I said. "I forgot how to."

"How to read?"

"How to want to."

He put the cup down and looked at me. Not searching. No pressure. Just present.

"Sometimes wanting comes back when you give it a chair."

I didn't know what that meant in words. But I felt it, the idea that longing doesn't need to be chased, only allowed to sit.

He grabbed the cloth again. I looked at him, then at the door.

"You close late," I said.

"I close when the room is empty," he said. "Not tonight."

Something inside me calmed down. Something changed again. It wasn't an attraction. I couldn't name the spark. It was the feeling of not being seen. The feeling of being able to sit still without having to earn it. His fingers didn't touch mine when he gave me the umbrella I had left by the door. In some way, I still felt warmer.

There was a song on the radio that I couldn't place. He turned the sound down, almost all the way off. The rain turned into a mist. Time went on and on.

After a while, he asked, "What do you do?"

I said, "Publishing. Reports and suggestions." A lot of numbers that look like words.

"And you?" I asked.

"I pour coffee. I pay attention. I read what people give me," he said, lifting one shoulder slightly. "It keeps a man honest."

He didn't say it in a smart way. I trusted him. I believed the room more than anything I had said about my life in the last few months.

I looked at the clock and got up. He grabbed the umbrella that I had propped up against the door. He held it out by the handle so that I wouldn't have to touch the wet fabric.

He said, "If the rain keeps up, bring it back tomorrow."

I said, "It always does."

"Yes, it does," he said. His smile was small and steady, the kind that doesn't take your attention away but gives it back.

I went outside. The bell above the door made that soft sound again. There weren't many people on the street. A thin river of water flowed along the curb. The cool night air touched my face and took something with it. I had no idea what.

I took the long way home. The metal grate on the corner newsstand was pulled down and locked. Even though the bakery was dark, the smell of sugar was still in the air. Like a guard who didn't plan to move, a cat watched me from a dry ledge under a balcony. Somewhere, a couple was fighting about everything and nothing at the same time. I didn't rush.

There is a florist below my apartment. The stairwell smells like peonies and ribbon in the spring. There was a smell of wet cardboard and rain tonight. I turned off the lights and put the umbrella in the bathtub to let it drip. The quiet in the room didn't feel threatening like it usually does. It was like an open book. I sat on the edge of the bed with my coat on and listened to the water hit the porcelain tiles in a slow, steady rhythm.

I told myself I was sleepy. I wasn't. I told myself that all I had to do was get coffee. That was almost right. I closed my eyes and saw the shelf with the old paperbacks on it. I could hear the radio through the rain. I saw how Giovanni listened before he spoke, as if he wanted words to come to him, not chase them.

I opened the window in the kitchen a little more. As I heated milk on the stove, cool air hit the steam coming from my cup. I don't know why I made milk at that time. It felt nice. I put it in a mug and stood by the sink.

People think that moving to a nice place will make everything better. No one is saved by Rome. It is a looking glass. It shows you paths that go back if you get lost. It gives you a piazza at dusk and a reason to stay until the lights come on if you're ready. I hadn't made up my mind about who I was. I only knew that I was sick of not being someone.

I came to Rome a long time ago with two suitcases and the kind of hope that stays with you. The job was only supposed to last six months, like a break between storms. But the city quietly pulled me in. I found out where the buses sleep at night. Which baker gives you the first warm *cornetti* without judging you. How to keep from crying on the subway. Silence became normal over time. Routine became a form of protection. I found out what my own quiet looks like.

It's easy to get lost in a life that seems to be going well. Advancements. A better seat. A group that claps when you give them the report that no one wanted to write. You tell yourself it matters when you get home late. You get up early and tell yourself that things will be different. Then, one night, you duck into a small room with books and coffee. That's when you remember that your life has a pulse that has nothing to do with calendars.

I washed the mug and put it upside down to dry. The rain coming from the umbrella had slowed down. I still left it there. The rain stopped outside, leaving the city shiny and quiet. A slow, careful hand closed a shutter. A church bell rang ten times and then stopped.

I leaned against the window frame and looked out. The street below was empty except for a stray cat that was grooming one wet paw very carefully. A lamp lit up a circle of pale gold on the stones. I could see the circle almost all the way to the corner where the street turns and the light goes out. I thought about the café, the bell, and how a stranger had said my name like it was no big deal.

You might know how this feels. The soft click that happens when a door inside you opens a little. Nothing big. No guarantees. There was only air where there was none. You take a breath. You know that you don't have to keep everything together all the time to deserve your next breath.

I shook the water off my coat and hung it on the back of a chair. I closed the window and left it unlocked. Even the refrigerator was quiet after the rain. I went to bed without turning on a light. The dark was nice. It felt like a story I hadn't learned how to tell yet. Maybe that's why the quiet asked so much of me.

I will take the long way to work again tomorrow. I'll walk by the little store to see if the sign says "Open." I'll tell myself it's for coffee. It could be for something else. Maybe for the part of me that wants to sit at a table where no one asks me to be anyone but myself.

Tonight, I will let the city live on its own. I'll put the questions on hold. I'll count the last drops that fall from the umbrella like slow steps.

I didn't know it then, but that little room had already changed how I was quiet. Nothing had been washed away by the rain. It only made the truth shine a little brighter in the streetlights. I could see just enough to take one more step.

I slept with the window open a little bit. The night smelled like stone, lemon, and the first clean page.

I didn't know it yet, but that little room would be where my life learned how to breathe again.

CHAPTER TWO

Sanctuary

The next week went by as some weeks do in Rome, getting longer or shorter depending on how close you are to your own thoughts. Work came in waves, just like always. Rain was always behind me. I kept telling myself that the night at Libri e Caffè was just a break from my normal life. But by Friday night, my feet were already taking me back there, steady and sure, as if they remembered something I had tried to forget.

I had lived in Rome long enough to know where my feet were taking me before my mind would let me admit it.

When I walked in, the bell above the door made a soft, forgiving sound. The warm air touched me softly, like a hand that I knew well. The smell inside was the same as it had been that first night. Coffee. Paper from a long time ago. A faint hint of citrus, like someone had cut a lemon and left the peel on a plate by accident. The rain behind me hit the glass softly, making it sound more like a memory than the weather.

The café was in that strange hour between afternoon and night, when time seems both close and far away. A chair made a soft noise as it moved across the wooden floor. Someone laughed once, quietly and to themselves. The pages turned at a slow, steady pace that helped calm a busy mind. It felt like the room had a heartbeat that wasn't mine but knew how I felt anyway.

Giovanni was behind the counter, sleeves rolled up to his elbows, polishing a small piece of wood as if it were the most important thing in the world. There was a tiny coffee stain on the inside of his wrist. I was curious if he still noticed it or if he had just gotten used to it. When he looked up and saw me, something soft passed between us. He didn't smile brightly or eagerly. It was calm and warm, the kind that you could feel in your eyes before you could feel it in your mouth.

He said, "Back again." His voice had a warmth that made you think he meant it.

"I guess the rain isn't the only thing that pulls me in," I said.

He tilted his head a little, as if he were listening for something more than what I said. "Then you're in good company."

I sat at the same table by the window. The wood was still warm from the person who had sat there before me. Giovanni went back to his quiet work, humming something that sounded more like a thought than a song. The café moved around him slowly and easily. A woman at the counter wrote in a little notebook. Long after the sugar had dissolved, a man stirred his coffee. The light on the walls was soft and golden, like a picture that had been left out in the sun.

For the first time in a long time, I didn't feel like I was invading my own silence. The sound of Rome after the rain reminded me of Lagos on some nights. Not in sound, but in spirit. There was a certain kind of music in Lagos. Very bright. Never-ending. A city that breathed deeply. I didn't always belong to it, but even here in this quiet Roman café, a part of me still felt its rhythm.

Giovanni came up to me with a small package wrapped in brown paper and tied with a thin string. I didn't get why he was being nice to me. I only knew that a part of me had been waiting for kindness without asking.

I asked, "What is this?"

"That was the event of the day," he said.

"What event?"

"Because I say so." His smile told me to meet him halfway. "Open it."

There was a first edition of *Jane Eyre* inside. Other hands had smoothed out the cover. The pages felt soft and alive. I couldn't breathe. He had written on the inside flap:

To Sophia, a kindred spirit who reminds me that even stories we know can still surprise us.

The words got blurry for a second. "Giovanni, this is too much."

He said, "It's not too much. Stories surprise us. Life does the same. It's a reminder."

He made me a cappuccino behind the counter, then came to sit across from me. We didn't talk for a long time. The noise in the café rose and fell like the tide.

"Do you read it a lot?" I asked.

"*Jane Eyre*? A lot," he said. "When I was a kid, I thought it was a love story. Later, I realized it was a story about staying alive and keeping your fire going even when the world tries to put it out."

His words hit me in a quiet place. I ran my fingers over the worn cover. "She reminds me of someone I used to know," I said.

"Then maybe you're remembering her," he said in a soft voice.

I opened a blank notebook when I got home that night. The page looked too clean and too ready. My hand stopped for a second. Then some lines that weren't straight came. Another one came after it. They weren't pretty. They didn't have to be. They showed that I was still alive.

The days that followed went by in a quiet way. The café turned into a safe place. Before work, I would stop for a cappuccino and read or just watch how the light changed on the floor. In the evenings, I came back again, drawn by the soft fading of the light and the warm hum of voices. The coffee and books were important, but they weren't what kept me there. It was how the room moved. People came in with things they couldn't name, and somehow the air made them feel lighter.

Giovanni walked through the room like someone who was okay with being quiet. He could remember names, books, and little things about how people liked their drinks. He made room without filling it. A student who was very busy studying. A woman in her seventies drawing a map of Florence. A couple arguing quietly and then laughing halfway through. He never cut in. He just listened.

One night after closing, he stood behind the counter and turned a cup in his hands. He said, "My dad once told me that listening is like a shelter." Then he put a single chestnut on the counter between us, as if to say that some stories only come when they are ready. He didn't say what the gesture meant. He didn't have to. The people in the room got it.

He stopped for a moment and rested his fingers lightly on the counter. In the silence, something felt deeper than talking.

"And you?" he asked, not with insistence but with curiosity that welcomed instead of pressed. "Where did you come from in the first place?"

I paused, not because I was scared but because memories can be heavy.

I said, "Nigeria. First Lagos, then Jos, before I left."

Giovanni nodded slowly, as if the name itself had a beat. He said, "A city with its own rhythm. I think it still lives inside you, even when you're far away from it."

His words echoed softly.

When the café got quiet and the lights hummed gently, I thought of Lagos nights when the power went out and neighbours would gather under the same moonlight to talk, laugh, tease, and stay alive. This room had the same feeling of belonging, where people could breathe the same air without having to say hello. Different continents. The same quiet pull of being close to someone.

I didn't say all of this out loud. But I knew that he would have understood.

I saw him finish his work, which took a long time. The café settled around him like a heart finding its beat.

People trusted him for no reason. Not because he filled the place with silence but because he respected it. He made your pauses seem natural, not like they were broken. Some people shine when they get attention. Giovanni stood out by making space for people to thrive. He was calm, and it felt like he had earned it. The kind of guy you want life to be nice to.

Weeks went by without a hitch. Then one morning, a note in Giovanni's handwriting appeared near the door:

Bring a book that made you a different person. Please tell us why.

The café looked warmer than ever that night. Old jars held candles that flickered. The smell of espresso, sugar, and lemon filled the air. Isabella was the first to arrive, loud and sure of herself. She brought a bottle of limoncello and *The Count of Monte Cristo.*

"To courage," she said as she poured without asking.

With a smile, Giovanni shook his head. "Always have courage with you."

"Balance," she said with a smile. "Someone has to keep your stories alive."

The room was full of laughter. People took turns talking about the books that changed their lives. I stood with *Pride and Prejudice* in my hands when it was my turn. My hands were sweating.

I said, "Elizabeth Bennet reminds me to stand my ground. Even when the world tells me not to."

For a moment, the room was silent. Then Isabella raised her glass to me. The applause was soft, but it felt like the start of something.

Giovanni leaned against the counter next to me when the room was finally empty. "You are building more than a story, Sophia," he said. "You are getting braver."

"I guess you're teaching me how," I said.

He smiled gently. "I just make the coffee. You do the rest."

I walked home that night through streets that were quiet. The smell of rain was still in the air. A soft golden glow came from a bakery window. There was music coming from a long way away. I remembered Giovanni's story about how his father taught him to listen. I thought about everyone who had come into the café and left feeling a little better.

I opened my notebook again when I got home. The page was full now. The city breathed outside my window, and for the first time in years, I did too.

That was enough for now.

CHAPTER THREE

Choices

The lights in the office above me hummed, a thin, tired sound that made everything seem even more faded than it already was. There were neat rows of grey cubicles, each with a person in it, blinking at a screen as if their eyes were doing the best they could. Someone's reheated pasta and burnt coffee made the air smell bad. Keys were tapped. Printers let out a sigh. People talked in polite tones that could have been about anything from spreadsheets to heartbreak. Everyone sounded asleep.

It was a life that kept going even when none of us inside it really did.

My own days had started to look like the rows of cubicles. Expected. Inside. Not quite in the right way. Deadlines, reports, and emails. I had left Nigeria years ago to start over and find room to breathe, but some days I wondered if I had just traded one pain for a slightly less painful one. Fifteen years of being reliable. Being helpful. Being the person who kept getting out of bed even when her body wanted to stay under the covers.

The job had been a lifeline for me after my divorce. A steady paycheck. A chair that had my name on it. A schedule that was strong enough to lean on. But what used to help me stay afloat had slowly become the thing that kept me from moving forward.

By late afternoon, my head would be ringing, and I would watch the clock on the wall like you watch rain through glass. Waiting for it to end. Waiting for the day to let me go.

The only time of day that felt like breathing was after sunset. Books and coffee. The smell of espresso and old paper was warm. The soft sound of wooden chairs scraping. The sound of pages turning over and over again. The emptiness inside me opened up enough to let light in for an hour or two.

Not every night. Some nights, even the café couldn't help me quiet my mind. Giovanni saw those nights. He always did, though.

He put a cappuccino in front of me and pulled out the chair across from mine one night.

He said, "You have been looking at the same page for twenty minutes. What is the truth behind that?"

I tried to smile. "Just a long day."

He said quietly again, "A long day or the same day again?"

The question got into a part of me that I had avoided for years. I laughed a little because I didn't know what else to do.

I said, "Maybe both."

He looked at me for a moment, his voice still soft. It felt like something inside me had been loosened up for years, and his words had turned the key.

"Then maybe it's time to start a new chapter."

I said, "It's not that easy."

He said, "Nothing real is easy. But that doesn't mean it can't be done."

There was a long silence between us. Not empty. Waiting. A thought that I had buried began to come back. A life that wasn't all about deadlines or showing how useful I was. A life that could be mine again.

"I think I want something else now," I said. I was shocked by the honesty. It was older than regret but younger than hope.

Giovanni nodded once, as if he had known what I was going to say before. "Dreams?" he asked.

I nodded. I remembered the girl I had been in Nigeria, standing in a busy bus station with too many hopes and not enough words to express them. I had learned how to stay alive, but I had forgotten how to want.

"Then turn the page," he said.

After he stood up to help another customer, I couldn't get his words out of my head.

He leaned against the counter next to my table when he came back. His voice dropped, as if he had opened a door that only a few people could see.

He said, "When I was a boy, my father worked a small brazier by the Tiber. Every winter, he wore the same apron. There was smoke in his hair. Hands warm from opening chestnuts for strangers. He whistled softly to himself. He whistled it every day, but I never learned the tune."

He stopped to clean a ring of coffee off the wood.

"He used to say that you could learn a lot about someone by looking at their hands. If a hand shakes, warm it up. Give space if someone is holding back. At that point, I wanted to leave Rome. It was too small, too heavy, and too loud."

He looked down and thought about it.

"He died all of a sudden," he said. "Not enough time to say goodbye. I didn't know how to deal with the stillness. I stood by the river and listened after the funeral. Listened very carefully. The city didn't try to hide its cracks. The walls didn't hide how old they were. Deep down, I knew that Rome wasn't something to be afraid of. It was a lesson."

He gently set the cloth down.

He said, "That's why I opened this place. Not to sell coffee but to give people a place to put down what they are carrying and take a break."

I felt a warmth in my chest. Not romantic. Not very dramatic. Humane. The kind that comes when someone looks at you in a way that feels strong enough to hold.

He said, "The hardest part is figuring out where to start. After that, the story goes with you."

That night, I took my time walking home. The city was getting ready for spring. The river breeze brought the faint smell of chestnuts and yeast from a bakery that was still open late. I put my bag down in my apartment and opened my notebook to a blank page. My chest felt tight, but I stayed still until the panic calmed down enough for one sentence to come out.

It wasn't pretty. It was mine.

I took the long way to work the next morning just to go by the store. Giovanni was on a ladder cleaning the tops of the shelves. He tapped the cover with one finger when he saw the notebook under my arm.

He said, "Writing isn't about making something perfect. It's about seeing what's already there."

His words were like a small, warm stone that I didn't know I needed.

Weeks went by like water does when you stop fighting it. The office stayed the same. The café kept its hum. I found a path I had never seen before between the two places. I started to notice little things. Giovanni put the cup down so quietly that it felt like he was showing respect. How he said hello to people by the names they gave their dogs. How he stopped before answering a question, as if he were waiting for the most honest answer.

One night, the open door let in the smell of chestnuts. Clouds began to form over the buildings. Giovanni was next to me in the doorway.

He said, "My father used to say the city speaks when the air is like this."

"What is it saying now?" I asked.

"Choose," he said. "Even if you decide to stay. Pick."

He wasn't asking for an answer. He was reminding me that I had one.

He didn't touch me when we said goodnight. He didn't have to. I could feel how soft he was all the way home. Intimacy doesn't always mean touching or kissing. Sometimes, it's the space someone makes for you when it's hard to breathe.

I filled a glass with water in my kitchen and watched the rim fog up with warmth. I thought about the years I had spent living a life that kept me safe but small. I thought of the twenty-four-year-old girl who entered a world that didn't know what to do with her and decided she would learn how to fit in anyway.

Choices. The word used to scare me. It felt like a key now.

I went to the window and left the notebook open on the table. The city let out a breath. A bell rang somewhere and counted to ten. I still didn't know what I wanted, but the page was no longer empty. I wasn't either.

Tomorrow I would go to work and do something useful. I would go back to the café tomorrow night and let the quiet calm me down. I had never walked that road before, but I could feel it taking shape under my feet.

I turned off the light and stood in the soft dark. You start making choices long before you say them out loud. It starts when you say you want more than just to live.

I wanted more.

You might not have earned your freedom.

Maybe it was something you finally let yourself go for.

CHAPTER FOUR

The Jump

Two months later, the letter lit up my screen.

To resign.

The word looked like it was the end, which made my throat feel tight.

The cursor blinked below it, as if to say, "Are you sure?"

No, I wasn't. I still printed it.

The machine made a lot of noise, more than it should have. Every time I dragged the paper, it felt like the world was changing its weight and moving on without me.

I had been thinking about this choice for years. After the divorce, the job was my safe place, the thing that kept me going when everything else fell apart. But what used to calm me down had slowly started to trap me. Safe. Expected. No air.

Fifteen years of coming.

Of being helpful.

Of cleaning up the messes that no one else wanted to deal with.

Of living in a routine so closely that it felt like a second skin.

I was in my mid-forties and woke up every morning feeling like I was twenty and seventy at the same time. I was young enough to want more but old enough to be afraid of the cost of getting it.

The office was busy as usual. Ringing phones. Keys were tapped. Someone quietly cursed at a printer that was stuck. People walked by me without knowing that I was ending something that had shaped almost all of my adult life.

A message from Giovanni popped up on my screen.

You don't have to see the whole staircase.
Take the first step.

My hands were sweaty on the letter. The name above my signature looked like it belonged to a different version of me, someone who was braver or more sure of themselves.

I thought about my first day here. I was twenty-four years old and still hurt from the divorce. I held on to a leather portfolio like it could keep me standing. When I walked in, the men in suits hardly looked at me. I felt like no one could see me until Mr. Daniels, my boss, cleared his throat.

"Men, this is Sophia. She is our new analyst." *Honestly, I'm more qualified than any of you.*

The room was quiet. I made myself smile.

"Then I guess I should do what I said."

A few people laughed. Most people didn't. But I still showed what I could do.

Late at night. Long reports. Silent wins.

I made a name for myself.

After that, I put up a wall.

I was ready to leave both of them now.

I knocked on Mr. Daniels' door. He looked up from a pile of contracts, and the fine lines around his eyes were deeper than I remembered.

"Sophia. What are you thinking about?"

I put the letter down. "I quit."

He read it once, then again, but more slowly. His mouth got tighter and then looser.

He said, "You've been here for a long time. You're not just a member; you are family."

I said softly, "That's why this is hard. But it's time."

He leaned back in his chair and let out a breath, as if he were letting go of something he had been holding on to for years.

He said, "The day you walked into that conference room with your leather portfolio, I knew you were going to change this place. Do you remember?"

"I do," I said. "I thought the table would swallow me whole."

He smiled. "You made it sit down."

We were both quiet for a moment. He pushed the letter toward me, giving me one last chance to reconsider. I didn't.

"Go and build the rest," he said. "You've earned it."

My legs felt both weak and strong when I left his office, like they do when you step off a ledge you've been thinking about for years.

The next two months went by in a flash. I taught my replacement how to do my job. Wrote down every step. Checked everything twice. People said I worked harder after I quit than before.

It was important to me to leave well.

On my last day, the team crowded into the break room with a cake from the store and coffee that wasn't very hot. Amanda hugged me so hard that my ribs hurt.

She whispered, "I can't picture this place without you. I'm proud of you."

David put a paper crown on my head to try to hide the tears in his eyes.

"Who's going to stop me from messing up every spreadsheet now?"

We took a picture in bad light, but I knew I would keep it.

I stayed behind to fold the tablecloth and stack the plates after the crowd left. Mr. Daniels came up next to me with two paper cups of coffee.

He said, "Thank you for leaving well."

"It was important to me."

"It shows."

He let me turn off the light.

I drove home without saying a word. The sun went down low, making the rooftops look golden. Rome looked different, not like it was changing, but like it was watching me change.

Libri e Caffè was my first stop. Giovanni had already put two cups on our table. Steam rose up like a soft blessing.

He raised his cup.

"To new beginnings."

I said, "To courage."

The sound of porcelain clinking was small and bright, like a bell that only I could hear.

Giovanni said, "You did it."

"I did."

I let out a breath. "I don't know what's next." A small fear curled in my stomach, reminding me that letting go still came with its shadows.

"You're not supposed to. That's how you know it's real."

That night, I sat at the table in my kitchen. The letter of resignation was folded up next to my laptop.

Giovanni once told me that it wasn't about leaving.

It's about letting go of the person you used to be so you can become the person you are now.

I opened a document with no text in it. My fingers hovered, not sure what to do. Then the words started to come, first slowly and then faster. Pieces. Little bits of memory. Thoughts that aren't fully formed. They didn't have to be perfect. They just had to be there.

For fifteen years, noise had been inside me.

I wasn't scared of the quiet for once.

Sometimes, the silence got too deep, and I thought about home—not just Nigeria but the younger me who thought she had to be twice as strong to be seen. Back then, being quiet was like armour.

Now it was a place to get better.

I was free.

There wasn't a lot of fanfare when freedom came.

It came quietly, right when I stopped asking for permission to change.

CHAPTER FIVE

Not Bound

Writing felt like breathing in the first few weeks after I left. There were no approvals. No deadlines. No slides. Only me and a blank page that didn't judge. I was forty-five years old, old enough to know that starting over was dangerous but still young enough to hope it wasn't too late. The age felt strange on me, like a coat I wasn't sure I had picked out.

Then the doubt came in. What if it isn't good? What if I'm not good? I didn't know what this was turning into. Fiction. Memory. Fragments. The field that was open began to feel heavy. The joy faded as my hopes grew. Still, I kept writing. Some days, the sentences came like rocks. I stopped some days because it hurt too much to be heard.

Giovanni and I sat on a worn-out bench in the park one evening, just before dark. There were kids laughing behind us. A dog chased a pigeon but then stopped. The leaves moved like the tide going out.

"I thought quitting would feel like starting," I said. "Instead, it feels like I left parts of me behind. My job was who I was. I don't know who I am without it. I remembered leaving Nigeria for Rome in the same way, thinking that once I set foot on new ground, I would magically know who I was meant to be. You can move to a new continent, but you can still feel in your heart like you owe someone money."

He looked at my face. He didn't hurry to fix the silence. He finally said, "You are free. Being free doesn't mean you're not safe. It means you finally let go of something that was too heavy." At first, it was hard to understand. Then it was clear. But freedom also gave me the chance to ask questions I had been avoiding for years, like who I was becoming and if a woman my age could start over without saying sorry.

"Maybe I was wrong," I said. "What if that office was the only place I really fit in?"

He said, "A title is not a belonging. Belonging is when you don't lie to yourself to stay. For the first time in years, you are choosing yourself. That's not being selfish. That takes guts."

"I told Daniels I trusted him. I was needed by the team. It feels like a failure to leave."

He said, "It is human. You took care of everyone else for so long that you forgot to take care of yourself. How long can someone hold a whole room before they fall?"

His words hit home. I thought about my marriage. For years, I tried to meet demands that got bigger every time I met them. If I put in more effort. If I loved more. If I gave it another shot. I had done the same thing at work. Nights that are late. Silent sacrifices. Proving and proving until there was no one left to show.

"I've tried my whole life to make things better," I said. "My marriage. My work. Me. It was never enough."

Giovanni put his hand on mine. Warm. Steady. "You were fighting battles that no one could win," he said. "Letting go is not a sign of failure. It is living. It is power."

The world got blurry. The stones got sharper again when I blinked. Something had broken when they left. I didn't know if it would get better.

I asked, "Does it get easier?"

"No," he said at first. He turned to look at the last light in the trees. "Then it starts to make sense. The choices that are hardest to make often give you the most freedom."

The lights along the path blinked on. A moth flew around one light and then flew into the dark. I put my hand in my coat pocket and found a folded receipt with just one word on the back.

Bravery.

I didn't remember writing it. I still kept it.

"I want to believe that I can make a life that feels like mine," I said.

He said, "You already are."

We sat down as the park got less busy. The silence felt like space, not emptiness. A small spark warmed me up. Not being tied down didn't mean being lost. It didn't mean falling. Maybe it meant learning how to fly.

CHAPTER SIX

The Page Turner

The list was on my kitchen table, waiting for me. Four lines that looked like doors.

Read Jane Eyre *in Italian.*

Write a book.

Go to a place I've never been.

Volunteer my time.

I ran my finger over the paper. These were not chores. They were parts of me I had put away while I survived.

I thought of the last years. Two suitcases. A one-way ticket. A marriage that made me feel empty. Rome took care of me when I had nothing to give. The job turned into a safe place. Then it became a habit. Then there was silence.

Now the city seemed to want more. Not to get better. To make.

My phone vibrated. A note from Giovanni.

It's always hard to write the first chapter. Just write it. Later, cappuccinos.

I smiled. He kept his faith when mine started to fade.

I took another look at the list. I didn't have to do everything. I need-ed one step.

Two days later, I was outside the community centre with my hand on the door. There was a flyer on the glass. *Program for Adults to Learn to Read and Write. People who want to help are welcome.* The happy font didn't match how I felt in my stomach.

What am I doing here? I'm not a teacher. What if I can't help?

I tightened the strap on my bag. The list helped me stay calm. Before I could change my mind, I pushed the door open.

The room smelled like pencil shavings and paper. Voices softly moved across the tables. Notebooks. Used paperbacks. Two kids in one corner were drawing pictures with short crayons.

"You must be Sophia."

I turned around. A woman with quick eyes and a cloud of red hair was already walking up to me.

She said, "I'm Clara. The person in charge. Giovanni said you would come by."

Of course, he had. Gratitude and annoyance came at the same time. Clara walked me through the room, pointing out people and telling me what they needed. I watched the students' faces as they sounded out the words. Moving lips. Fingers tapping on paper. Effort filled the room like music.

She stopped at a table in the back. "You will work with Mateo," she said. "He has been coming for a few weeks now. He is doing fine. He needs words."

Mateo looked up. Hair that was silver. Posture that was straight. Eyes that were nervous. He put his hands on a thin paperback book like it might fly away.

I sat in front of him. "Hi, Mateo. My name is Sophia. Clara said we would work together."

He said carefully, "Sophia. I'm not good with words."

I said, "That's okay. We'll take our time. We will get there together."

We got started. His voice shook at first. He stopped and said he was sorry. I told him he didn't have to say sorry. We talked about the hard parts. We put circles around the words that were important to him. When a sentence surprised us, we laughed. His voice steadied by small amounts. The pauses got shorter. The shame in his eyes became clearer.

He closed the book and looked at me. "Thank you," he said, quiet and clear. "I didn't think I could."

"You did," I said. "And you did it so well." I put the notebook between us. "Give me a word you want to own."

He thought for a long time. "Belong," he said.

We wrote it slowly, letter by letter, until it looked like it had always been his.

Giovanni put a cappuccino on the table at Libri e Caffè that night and sat down across from me.

"So," he asked, "how did it go?"

I said, "It was good," and then I let out a breath I hadn't realized I was holding. "I thought I would be the one to help him. I believe he helped me. His words made the room feel bigger, like life still had possibilities that I had quietly put out of reach."

He said, "That's how it works. You give. You find yourself."

The next morning, I went to the library next to the centre. A bright spine on a low shelf caught my eye. *How to Tell Your Story. A guide for beginners.* I held it as if it were heavier than paper.

The first line on the first page read, "Every great story starts with one sentence. Put it down on paper. The rest will follow."

It seemed like the book was talking only to me.

I signed up for a card and borrowed it after my session with Mateo. That night, I opened my notebook and put my pen down. I sat there and waited.

A woman thought that it was never too late to start over.

I read the line once. Then two times. My heart beat faster. The words weren't perfect. They didn't have to be. They belonged to me. For the first time in years, I could see the faint outline of a future I had stopped imagining, one with chapters I thought I could no longer hope for.

I kept coming back in the weeks that followed. Pages came together. There was also a question I couldn't ignore anymore. What would happen if I not only wrote, but also lived like a writer?

CHAPTER SEVEN

Setting Out

The rain made a soft sound on the tall windows of Libri e Caffè. I stood by the window and watched the street shine. It had been a week since we'd called the Storytellers' Showdown. Three months of making plans. A single night of bravery. The room was still in my mind.

If I stood very still, I could hear the laughter. Not the kind that hides. The kind that lets go. But the laughter didn't last. What stayed were the stories.

Clara, the program coordinator, stood in the middle in a dress she had bought at a thrift store that looked like it belonged on stage. She called herself Elizabeth for three minutes. She then put the voice down and spoke as Clara. The room leaned toward her like a body does when it's hot. The applause felt good when she was done.

Next was Mateo. He held his book like it was a promise. His first words were soft and almost lost in the sound of milk hissing at the espresso machine. He kept going. His voice got louder. He was smiling through his tears by the end.

Enzo wore a crooked paper pirate hat and yelled his last line so loudly that the doorbell shook. He bowed like a king. His mom cried into her hands.

The performances weren't perfect. They were proof. For a moment, I thought about how many chapters of my own life I had put off because I thought I wasn't ready. But I was learning that being ready is something you grow into, not something you wait for. People can talk while holding heavy things. Dreams don't end in silence. Being vulnerable can make a room feel stronger than fear.

Doubt came back in the weeks that followed, as it always does. What if you don't succeed? What if you look dumb? The questions flew around like birds that didn't want to land.

I walked around my apartment at night, looking at the map on the wall. Faded pins showed where I said I would go. For years, I had wanted to travel. I always had an excuse not to go. The students need me. It is not safe by itself. I was scared and called it useful.

There was a quiet voice under the noise. Mateo's steady breathing. Clara's hands were open. Enzo's loud shout. They were also scared. But they went anyway. It hit me then how many lives we never think about for ourselves because we think the door is already closed. But some doors stay open for years.

One afternoon, Giovanni put a cappuccino in front of me and sat down in the chair across from me.

At the age of forty-five, I was learning that reinvention wasn't just for young people. The idea didn't arrive with confidence, it arrived softly, like something I had been avoiding without realizing it. He said, "You have been looking out there for a long time."

I said, "I've been thinking about going on a trip."

His eyebrows went up. He smiled. "Finally. I was getting worried that you would wait forever."

"I kept waiting for the right moment," I said. "I don't think it exists. No one is going to let me do it."

He said, "You make the perfect time. Where are you going?"

I stopped. My heartbeat once against my ribs. I said, "Out of Rome first," I said. "I don't know what comes after. Somewhere. All over."

He lifted his cup. "Not waiting."

I raised mine. "Not waiting."

The next week was full of lists and small panics. I got ready. I took everything out. I picked a train that went more slowly. I made reservations for small rooms off-season. I made a list of friends who might be able to lend me a couch. In Rome, favours are a type of money. Giovanni helped me make a fair trade.

He insisted on a simple toast at the café before I left. He raised a glass of prosecco.

"To new beginnings," he said.

The air felt different the moment I arrived, as if the city had been waiting to see who I had become. The warm air smelled like oranges and salt. There was a lot of noise in the streets from the markets. Fish on ice. Tomato pyramids. Espresso hissing from carts. The city welcomed me with open arms and let me walk right in.

I met Marco, a historian who liked stories more than facts, on a terrace one night. He talked with his hands, and the city seemed to rise and fall with them. He pointed to a chipped cornice and told me about three lives that had gone by it. He put a lemon leaf in my notebook.

He said, "For luck. For pages you haven't written yet."

He said he would take me to Palermo the next day. I agreed. We walked by saints carved into stone and paint that had faded, as well as balconies with laundry that waved like flags. He loved his city like someone loves a song they heard as a child. I told him about the students, Rome, and Libri e Caffè.

He said, "You should write this down," over tiny cups of espresso. "You see it in a different way."

His words hit home and stayed.

From Palermo, I went to the Valley of the Temples in Agrigento. The ruins rose from the earth like old bones that still remembered how to stand. The cicadas buzzed. The air was still. I put my palm on a warm stone and felt a faint grit stick to my skin, as if time itself wanted to come with me.

Then Marco told me to do something crazy. Jumping out of a plane. Maybe I needed to prove to myself that fear no longer made my decisions for me.

The world got bigger when the door of the plane opened. My heart raced. The wind howled.

"Ready?" he asked, sounding calm as if we were about to step off a curb.

I held the harness and nodded. After that, I jumped.

The air rushed by. No weight. Free. My throat was full of fear and joy, which made one sound. There was no story for a few seconds. Just the sky. The chute opened up. The earth slowly rose to meet me, which was nice for once. I felt grass under my feet. I fell to my knees and laughed in a way I hadn't in years. It sounded like someone was opening a door from the inside.

I packed my small suitcase again that night. Sicily had given me more than I had asked for. Friends who are new. A risk I didn't think I would take. A reminder that beauty can be found in the unknown.

The next morning on the train north, I opened my notebook and wrote down everything I wanted to remember before it faded.

Florence. Siena. Back to Rome. I whispered the names to myself, as if saying them would make me brave.

The page didn't seem empty anymore. It felt like I was finally opening a door. Morocco had been mentioned long before it was decided. Giovanni talked about it the same way he talked about books he loved: without trying to convince anyone or rushing them. A place where colour didn't have to say sorry, where silence could still be loud, and where no one already knew anything about me.

I didn't say yes right away. I let the idea sit between us, growing quietly and not asking for anything. I didn't agree because I felt ready. It was because it was starting to feel harder to stay than to leave.

A few weeks later, the landscape changed.

CHAPTER EIGHT

The Tuscan Way

The train hummed north from Sicily, and the sea turned into fields. The rhythm of the rails had a soft, steady beat, like the world was breathing under me. I saw green and yellow patches of land being sewn together. Vineyards ran along the hills like careful writing. Cypress trees stood still and dark at the edges, watching over the afternoon in silence.

I put my forehead against the window. The glass was cool, and the train's low vibration felt like a slow heartbeat going through me. My journal was open on my lap, and the pages were a little curled from the salty air of the coast. The ink from earlier that day was still wet. I ran my finger over the words.

I'm learning to have faith in the unknown.

I learned that curiosity can calm fear in Sicily.

Tuscany makes you feel like you belong, even if only for a little while.

The hills were soft in the morning light, and they slowly opened up. It made me think of peaceful holidays in Jos during harmattan, when the sky turned faded pastels at dusk and time was free to go where it wanted.

The writing was uneven, as if it were shy. But the words seemed real.

An older couple sat close together on the other side of the aisle. They passed the orange slices back and forth, touching each other's hands. Each movement was slow and easy, like a language that didn't need sound. I smelled a faint citrus scent and felt something inside me relax.

The woman smiled at me, the kind of smile that doesn't ask for anything. I smiled back, even though it was small. She put her head on the man's shoulder as the train went around the first line of hills. For a short time, the world was just warmth, movement, and silence.

The ground outside started to rise and fold. The air looked golden because it was full of sunlight. Small farmhouses popped up, their walls light against the fields. There was smoke coming from short chimneys. The wind blew laundry on lines, making white shirts, a red dress, and a blue towel look holy as they moved in the light.

The train slowed down as it got closer to a small station. The sign said, "San Gimignano Sud." I picked up my bag, and the wheels made a soft clicking sound on the metal floor. The platform smelled like dirt and rain when I got off. A violin played softly in the background, with one note hanging on for too long, shaking between beauty and pain.

The town waited on the other side of the tracks, where the roofs were uneven and warm from age. I walked slowly, and my suitcase bumped over the cobblestones. A cat ran across the street with its tail up. Somewhere close by, bells rang the hour slowly and surely, as if time moved slowly here.

The air was full of smells, like baked bread, crushed rosemary, and smoke from far away. I saw a man sliding loaves into the oven through the fogged window of a small bakery. He brushed oil on the golden crust, which made it shine. I thought about it for a second, then pushed the door open.

The warmth inside wrapped around me. The baker looked up, smiled, and said, "Buongiorno, signora." His voice was soft but happy.

I said, "Buongiorno," and my accent was bad but nice.

He gave me a piece of focaccia that was still warm from the oven. "Assaggia," he said. Taste.

The bread melted in my mouth, and there was salt, olive oil, and something sweet underneath. I laughed quietly, and he smiled even more.

He wrapped another piece in brown paper and put a sprig of rosemary inside when I paid. He said, "For luck."

The air felt softer outside. I took the bread with me like a small gift from the day.

A few blocks later, I stopped at a café shaded by an awning the colour of cream. The chairs were made of wood and were smooth. I ordered panna cotta, and when it came, it was in a glass and shook a little. It was covered in dark syrup. The first bite was smooth and sweet. I closed my eyes and let it go away. It tasted like peace.

Two men at the next table were arguing about football in fast Italian. A woman read a newspaper while wearing sunglasses on her head. A dog was sleeping under a chair, and its paws were moving in a dream. Life moved at the slow pace of breathing. I felt like I was matching it.

The food here was more than just about taste. It was a way of being, a way of talking. Tuscany didn't talk to you; it showed you what it had to offer: bread, warmth, and time.

I found the bookshop in the late afternoon.

Libri Antichi e Amici was written on the sign above the door. The paint had faded, and the wood was smooth from years of use. The air inside smelled like dust, paper, and the faint sweetness of old glue. As I walked in, a bell rang softly.

Behind the counter was a woman with silver hair. She was wearing a loose linen lavender-coloured dress and shawl. She smiled and looked up from her book. "Good evening," she said.

I said, "Buonasera."

In a voice that didn't ask a question, she said, "You are not from here."

"No," I said. "From Rome."

She gave a nod. "Then you know. Each city has its own quiet. Florence keeps hers at night. Tuscany hides hers among the olive trees."

Her words wrapped around me like a blanket. I smiled but didn't know what to say.

She pointed to the shelves. "Go. Look around. The books will tell you which ones want to be held."

I walked around the narrow aisles. My fingers ran over the cracked leather spines and the paper that was soft at the edges. The quiet was alive, the kind that pays attention.

Then I saw it: a first edition of *Jane Eyre*. The cover was almost the same as the one Giovanni had given me. For a short time, time seemed to fold in on itself. I could almost hear his voice again, low and sure: "Stories surprise us." Life does the same thing.

I stood very still, and the memory was like a heartbeat in my chest.

I bought a small postcard with a watercolour of the Tuscan hills at the counter. I sat by the window and started to write. Dust floated in the air like light.

To Giovanni,

You read Tuscany with your whole body. Every piazza and vineyard feels like a new story. I can't stop thinking about you. When I get home to Rome, I'll tell you everything.

I paused, pen hovering. The ink trembled slightly in my hand. Then I smiled and tucked the postcard into my journal. I didn't post it. Some words, I realized, are meant only to be written.

The woman gave me a small bookmark before I left. "To help you remember who you are," she said.

The sun had moved low in the sky, and the streets were gleaming with gold. The hills behind the rooftops looked like they were full of light.

Days fell into a pattern that felt like breathing.

The smell of espresso and the sound of olive leaves moving outside my window woke me up in the morning. I walked on narrow paths through groves where wild thyme and rosemary brushed my hands. I saw farmers taking care of vines and women hanging sheets that flapped in the wind like sails. They smiled at me in a way that needed no words.

In the afternoons, I climbed the steep streets of nearby hill towns. When I stopped to rest, the stones felt cool under my hands. I stayed in piazzas where kids chased pigeons and old men played cards in the shade.

I sometimes had lunch at little trattorias that were high up in the valleys. I would sit for hours with a bowl of pici pasta and a glass of Chianti, and the world would open up in front of me. The wine weighted and waited. The pasta was soft and real. There was no rush. There was enough of everything.

My journal started to fill up quickly. I drew pictures of light on stone walls, wrote down the smell of basil drying in doorways, and wrote down things people said that stuck with me.

One old man told me as he trimmed vines by the road, "Life is slower here. That's how it lasts longer."

Every night, I would go back to my room and read what I had written that day. They didn't seem like stories. They felt like pieces of breath.

I rented a bike from a small shop near the square one afternoon. The man who gave it to me told me about the hills and smiled when I laughed. The road twisted and turned through the countryside, going past open fields and rows of vines. Sunflowers turned their heads to follow the light. A patch of red poppies stood out against the green at the edge of one field.

The air was dry and warm. The sound of insects buzzing got louder and quieter. Every time I turned the pedals, my mind got clearer. The rhythm of the movement calmed the noise in my head. I rode for a long time without thinking about the time. I could only feel the wind on my face and the steady pull of the ground under my tires.

I leaned the bike against a tree and sat on the grass when I stopped. I took off my shoes and felt the cool ground under my feet. I shut my eyes. The sound of birds and the distant murmur of the town came to me like a song I almost remembered.

For a short time, I didn't think about the past or the future. Just the slow, kind now.

That night, I climbed a hill that looked out over a large area of vineyard. As the sun went down, the land glowed and the leaves turned into gold coins. The shadows got longer. The sky shifted from amber to rose, then deepened toward violet.

I sat there with my knees pulled up to my chest. The air smelled like ripe grapes and dry grass. The light gently touched everything, like a hand brushing hair away from a face.

I thought about Giovanni, Marco, the students at the centre, and all the other people who had left their marks on the story of who I was becoming. They had all taught me something about being, staying, or leaving.

I realized that Tuscany was teaching me how to trust. There could still be parts of my life that were waiting to happen, parts I hadn't even thought of yet. There was no reason to be afraid of the unknown. I was learning how to walk through it.

A tear fell down my cheek, not because I was sad but because I felt a deep sense of relief. The pain of holding on was getting better. I put my hand on the rough, cool ground next to me and said, "Thank you."

No one answered, but the wind changed direction slowly, as if it had heard.

I was curious about what I would say to Giovanni about Tuscany. I also wondered what he would hear in the quiet spots between my words, where change was starting to happen. The next morning, I put my clothes in my small suitcase. The act felt heavier than I thought it would. It had never been easy to leave, but this time it felt different. Tuscany was more than just a place. It was a mirror that showed me what peace looked like when I stopped looking for it.

I zipped up the suitcase and sat on the edge of the bed for a moment. Something lighter, anticipation, met the ache in my chest. The world was waiting like a page ready for ink beyond this hill and this town.

The platform at the station sparkled in the early light. When the train got there, I got on and found a window seat. The engine started to hum, and the hills rolled by. The vineyards disappeared, the cypress trees shrank, and soon the sky opened up.

I put my hand on the glass. The sunlight hit my reflection, which was soft around the edges. I smiled to myself.

"I am ready," I said softly, almost afraid to break the silence.

The words didn't repeat. They made a deal. They settled. They belonged.

The sky opened up into morning as the train turned north toward Rome. The sound of the rails calmed my heart. The train took me forward as the story of my life kept opening up, one page at a time.

CHAPTER NINE

The Return to Rome

The train slowed down when it could see the first rooftops of Rome. They rose unevenly from the horizon, looking familiar but softer in the morning light. From a chimney far away, smoke curled up, and for a moment, it felt like the whole city was breathing out.

I put my hand on the window. The hills of Tuscany were gone behind me, but their calm stayed with me like a pulse under my skin. The sound of the rails got softer and softer until it was just a whisper. People around me started to grab their bags, and their voices started to mix in quick Italian. In the narrow aisle, a thousand small stories collided. I didn't stand up until the last minute.

When the doors opened, I felt the warm smell of coffee, exhaust, and rain on stone from Rome. Termini Station was full of life and movement. The sound of shoes on marble, train whistles, and luggage wheels banging on the floor. A year ago, this sound would have made my heart race. It felt like music today.

The city was its usual chaotic self outside. Vespas zipped between buses, vendors shouted out the prices of their fruit, and pigeons flew in circles over fountains like they were practicing an old dance. The sky above the rooftops was pale and clear after the rain. I stood on the steps for a while with my suitcase next to me and watched as the crowd moved in a way that had nothing to do with order and everything to do with rhythm.

Rome was still the same. But I had been gone for almost a month, which was long enough for the hills and coastlines to leave their marks on me but not long enough for Rome to forget me. I started walking without thinking. The wet pavement made a soft clicking sound when I walked. The streets I knew met me with their usual indifference, but I could feel something soft underneath it, a pulse of recognition, as if the city was watching to see what I had brought back.

I bought a cornetto and coffee at a small kiosk near the piazza. The man behind the counter, whose face I almost remembered, handed me the paper cup without my having to ask. "Bentornata," he said. *Welcome back.*

The words hit harder than they should have.

I sat down with my coffee at the fountain's edge. Water spilled in thin arcs over the marble, making a steady, cool sound. A little boy leaned over the edge and tried to touch the stream. His mother laughed softly behind him. The moment caught me by surprise. It was normal, short, and beautiful.

I used to rush through moments like this when I first got to Rome. Always reaching for something in front of me, scared to stand still long enough to feel where I was. Now I knew better. Stillness had shown me a different kind of movement.

As it pulled up to the curb, a bus hissed and let out a cloud of diesel and noise. I saw it leave, then turned onto the street that led to Trastevere. The sound of my suitcase rolling behind me was small and steady.

As I walked, the city changed. The wide boulevards turned into narrow lanes made of cobblestones. The walls got closer, and the plaster started to peel, showing layers of colour like ochre, rose, and pale blue. Laundry hung between the windows like flags from a country that wasn't there. I walked by the little church where I used to stop on rainy days and the bakery whose smell used to draw me in on the loneliest afternoons.

Every place felt like a note in a song I had forgotten I knew.

The air got cooler when I got to the river. The Tiber moved slowly under the stone bridges. It was heavy and quiet. I stood there for a while, watching the water fold and shine. My reflection shook at the surface, older, softer, and more sure.

Rome didn't ask questions. It just waited for you to find yours.

I crossed the bridge and went back to the neighbourhood I had left. The streets were smaller and the sounds were softer here. In the doorway, a cat stretched. Someone upstairs was playing a guitar, and the music stopped and sounded nice. At the end of the street, the familiar sign for Libri e Caffè appeared. The letters were faded by the sun and time. My heart raced.

I stopped for a second. When I saw the bookstore, memories came flooding back so strongly that I almost turned away. The smell of espresso, the sound of people talking, and Giovanni's voice all lived here.

But I was not the same woman who had first come in.

I moved forward.

As I walked in, the bell above the door rang softly. The sound wrapped around me like a memory. The shelves were full of books, the counter was full of cups and notes, and the soft amber light made the air feel like honey. But there were some small changes, like new books in the window, a different way the chairs were arranged, and a small vase of fresh lavender on the counter.

There was a young woman I didn't know standing behind the espresso machine. She smiled to say hello. She said, "Buongiorno."

I said, "Buongiorno." It was like hearing a song I knew after a long time of not hearing it.

I found my old seat by the window, in the same corner where I had read *Pride and Prejudice* and where Giovanni had put that first edition of *Jane Eyre* in front of me. As I sat down, the chair creaked. There was still a small scratch on the edge of the table where I had dropped my pen. The city moved past the glass, and the reflections of people and colours changed like waves.

I ordered a cappuccino, and when it came, I held the warm cup in my hands. The foam left a light mark on my lip, and I smiled at the memory of all the mornings that had started this way.

I could see the back of the store from where I was sitting. Someone was putting books on shelves. A man who was tall and moved slowly. I knew that posture before I knew the face. Giovanni.

He grabbed a stack of novels and straightened their spines until they were all in line. His hair had gotten a little longer. He had rolled up the sleeves of his shirt to his elbows. I could still feel his stillness, that quiet attention he carried like an anchor, even from this distance.

My heart raced, but not because I was scared. I knew who it was. He hadn't seen me yet. I could have yelled, but I didn't. I wanted to look for a while and take in how simple it was that he was there.

Then, he turned around and talked to the girl at the counter. She laughed at something he said, and he smiled in that small, almost shy way that always made me wonder what was going on in his head.

And all of a sudden, I knew that what I had brought back from Tuscany wasn't just peace. It was bravery. The kind that doesn't need big gestures, just quiet honesty.

I took my notebook out of my bag and opened it. The pages were full of ink, drawings, and bits of thoughts from all the places I had been. I turned to one that was blank. The paper had a faint smell of rosemary from the sprig I had kept.

I started to write:

I'm back. The city is louder than the hills, but my heart stays steady. I came back not to look for what I lost, but to give what I found.

I stopped and listened. Giovanni's voice was low, warm, and clear, and it could be heard faintly through the space.

I wrote again:

There are times when things just don't end. They wait for us to be ready to live them.

The words settled down on the page.

I looked up. Giovanni was walking toward the counter with a tray of cups in his hands. He looked up, and for a moment our eyes met across the room. His face changed from surprise to something deeper, like relief.

He didn't say anything. I didn't either.

He put the cups down and nodded once, slowly and honestly, as if no time had passed at all. The air between us felt lighter than it had in a long time.

I smiled enough. Sure enough.

He gave it back.

That was it. And that was enough for now.

I looked out the window again. The city moved like a movie projected on a wall. Kids crossed the street, a woman carried flowers, and the river sparkled just beyond the rooftops. I felt both inside and outside of it, like I was standing at the edge of my own story, ready to jump in.

The warmth of my coffee grounded me as I drank it.

For the first time since I left, I knew I wasn't looking anymore. The pain that used to fill me had turned into something soft, an openness to whatever would come next.

Rome was still the same. But I could finally see it for what it was, not what I wanted it to be.

I took my pen back up and wrote the last line:

I'm home.

The light outside moved across the cobblestones, making them look like gold. The bell over the door rang again when someone came in, and the quiet murmur of voices rose and fell. Life went on as usual.

I put my notebook away and rested my hand on its cover. The pages inside felt alive, as if they were breathing with every step, choice, and moment that had brought me here.

Some stories don't end with closure; they end with continuation.

Mine was still going on.

CHAPTER TEN

The City Wants to Know the Truth

Morning slid over the shelves like a gentle hand. I didn't plan to come back so soon, but my feet took me to Libri e Caffè without asking me first. The bell rang softly, and the room welcomed me like water welcomes a stone. There were more voices than yesterday. Regulars were talking in low tones, a few students were discussing, and an old man was reading the paper with a magnifying glass. The air smelled like coffee beans, lemon peel, paper, and wood polish. It had only been two days since I got back to Rome, but the city was already putting me to the test to see how honest I was willing to be with myself.

Giovanni was behind the counter with his sleeves rolled up and a cloth tucked into his hip. He was talking to the young barista and showing her how to tilt the pitcher to make the milk silky. He looked up as I got closer. He smiled simply and completely, like someone who is happy to see someone else. No fuss. No show.

He said, "Bentornata, Sophia."

Hearing him say my name calmed me down. "Good morning," I said. "The city is loud today."

"It likes to announce your return," he said, pointing to the corner. "Your seat is open."

He made the cappuccino himself. He always knew how to make little things feel like love and not like work. The cup came to my table warm, and the foam had a heart shape that looked like it wasn't planned. When I picked it up, the smell of cinnamon and heat hit me like a breath.

He asked, "How was the road?" and then sat down in the chair across from mine for a moment between orders.

I told him about Sicily. The air smells like orange blossoms. The noise in the market that sounded like a hymn. The Valley of the Temples going quiet all of a sudden. I told him about Tuscany, how the hills made my heart race, and how a woman in a bookstore put a sprig of rosemary in a paper bag like it was a blessing. His face didn't look like it was trying to move as I spoke. It just listened. That's a kind of wonder in itself.

"And you," I said, "has Rome been good to you?"

He tilted his head. "As nice as Rome can be. It gives you light and truth. The rest is up to us."

The bell rang. He stood up, said "Excuse me," and went back to the counter. I saw him greet people by name and remember their last book, favourite pastry, and how they liked their sugar. He moved like someone who had learned that love is shown through attention.

I opened my notebook. The page waited, but I didn't have the patience to wait. I wrote a line, then another, then stopped and listened to what was going on around me. Near the travel section, someone laughed. The old man sighed when he saw a headline. A kid carefully traced letters on the fogged-up window with one finger. It all felt like the city was talking to me in small, clear words.

Giovanni came back with two glasses of water and a small plate of almond biscotti when the rush was over. He gave me one and kept one for himself. We ate in silence, with the crunch of the food between us.

"Walk later," he said, not a question.

I nodded. "Yes."

We left the store in the kind of light that Rome likes to keep to itself. Last night's rain had washed the street clean, and the cobblestones shone in uneven squares. He locked the door, put the key in his pocket, and we started to move through the narrow streets that open and close like thoughts.

We weren't in a hurry. You can't rush through Trastevere. It likes to take its time. We walked by a tailor's shop where a suit was hanging on a form, half-finished. We walked by a small shrine built into a wall. There were flowers in a broken vase and a candle that flickered even in the light of day. We walked by a fruit seller who called out Giovanni's name and handed him a fig with a nod. He cut it in half and gave me the sweeter half. The seeds popped in my mouth. The flavour was like dirt and sunlight.

"Tell me what changed," he said as we walked over the bridge. The Tiber moved slowly beneath us.

"I stopped trying to put my life together like a puzzle," I said. "I began to see it as a place where I could live."

He smiled at the river. "Good."

On the other side, we walked through streets that felt like they were in a story. The wind picked up the laundry and dropped it again. Like mothers do with love, a woman watered geraniums in a clay pot and let a little spill into the street. A dog slept outside a bar under a chair, its ears twitching for no reason.

I talked in bits and pieces, which is how memory likes it. I told him about skydiving, how the drop and the roar made fear and joy feel the same for a few seconds. He laughed quietly, then looked shocked.

"You," he said. "You jumped out of a plane."

I said, "I did," and I could hear the pride in my voice. "I didn't know I could until I got there."

We got to Campo de' Fiori just as the market was closing. Stalls were being taken down, leaves were being swept off of tabletops, and crates were being stacked. The last flowers looked a little tipsy because of the heat. A woman with strong arms and a red scarf around her hair sold me three sunflowers for a coin and a smile. I held them up like a small flag.

We found a café with tables outside and sat down at one of them. He got an espresso for himself and a bottle of mineral water for me. We sat and watched the day end its shift. The square got smaller. A kid pulled a kite behind them like a pilgrim. The bronze statue in the middle didn't say anything.

He said, "You are writing."

"I am," I said. "More than I have in years. It isn't neat. It doesn't know what it is yet. It breathes."

He said, "That's all that matters. Breathing comes before singing."

The waiter brought a small bowl of green olives and a plate of salted almonds. We took our time eating. I told him about the adult literacy classes, Mateo, and how a grown man's face changes when he finally understands a sentence. Giovanni listened the way he always does, as if a story is a living thing that you don't want to scare.

He said after a while, "Stories aren't fun. They're how we help each other."

He paid the bill and shook his head gently when I offered him a coin. We walked again. The light had dimmed by then, and it looked like a shawl over the city. We walked by a violinist at the fountain's corner. She played the first few notes of a song that tasted like salt and sleep. A couple stopped and leaned against each other, as if the music had reminded them to remember.

We chose the quieter path near the river again. This path has stone steps that go down to the lower walk. There was dark, slow water close by that smelled faintly of iron and time. The wind blew without any trouble. He put his hands in his pockets. I put a piece of hair behind my ear and let the quiet do its job.

Finally, he said, "You look different. Not in your face. At your own pace."

"I feel different," I said. "The world is the same." *No, it isn't, not really.*

We stood there for a while with our elbows on the railing, not touching, sharing the view like people share bread. A small boat went under the bridge, leaving a V-shaped wake that made a short map on the water's surface. The buildings on the other side of the river turned the colour of apricots as the sun went down.

"Come eat," he said. "There's a trattoria on a side street where the owner has never lied to me. He makes pasta that makes up for all sins. We're going to eat and talk, and we won't act like time has rules."

He didn't say it just to fill space. He said it like a gift on a table.

I said, "Yes."

We went back to Trastevere. He took me down a street I had never seen before, past a door that opened to a courtyard where a lemon tree had decided to grow. The small trattoria smelled like tomatoes that had been sleeping in oil and garlic all afternoon. A man with a kind face greeted Giovanni by putting one hand on his shoulder and the other over his heart.

We had a simple salad with thinly sliced fennel on top. We shared a plate of *cacio e pepe* that was both simple and perfect. He poured red wine into my glass and then water. The conversation moved slowly, just like the walk did. He told me about the new volunteers at the café's reading nights, a retired teacher who had started a poem column on the bulletin board, and a regular who always returned books with a flower pressed at page thirteen for luck.

I told him about the postcard I wrote while I was in Tuscany but never sent. He reached across the table and drew a small circle on the wood with his finger, as if to show where that admission should go.

"You kept it," he said.

"I did," I said. "Some words are not for the post."

We ended with a small bowl of lemon sorbet that tasted like cold sunlight. He paid again when the bill came, and I didn't argue because the night felt like a gift, and arguing with a gift kills the music.

The air outside had gotten cooler. The streets were full of life in the way they are when night isn't too heavy yet. We walked toward the bookstore without even thinking about it. Our shadows followed us like patient animals.

He stopped at the door of Libri e Caffè and turned to me. The window showed both of us and the shelves behind us. The smell of coffee that never quite goes away came from inside.

He said, "Tomorrow. Come early. You need to sort through a box of old books. I won't act like it's not work. But it's good work. It will let us keep talking without having to look for reasons."

"I'll come," I said. It was easy to be sure.

He raised his hand as if to tuck a loose strand of hair behind my ear, but then he let it drop. The almost touch meant more than the actual touch would have. He didn't hurry. I didn't ask him to. We stood there for a short time until the night began to breathe.

He said, "Sleep well, Sophia."

"You too," I said.

I walked home with the city under my feet, like a tide under a boat. The smell of basil and something sweet came in through an open window. A woman slowly hung a small towel on a balcony. A cat walked in front of me and didn't look back. I held the three sunflowers like a promise I could keep.

I put water in a jar and put the flowers on the table in my apartment. I washed my hands and watched the soap slide off, a little ritual I didn't know I needed. Then I sat down and opened my notebook.

The words came in without knocking.

I wrote about how the river kept its slow life going. I wrote about the market closing like a theatre that had done its best for the day. I wrote about how Giovanni listens. People often hear it. It is uncommon to be heard without a request to act. I wrote a sentence about how cacio e pepe tastes and turned it into a prayer for simplicity.

I stood up and opened the window when my hand got tired. Night fell on the rooftops like a soft blanket. A violin somewhere kept playing the same note over and over until it found the right one. Someone on the street below laughed and then stopped, as if they had just remembered where they were.

I touched the postcard from Tuscany. I didn't send it then either. I put it in the back of my notebook and closed the cover.

I slept with the window open. The air tasted like stone and lemon, like Rome does when it forgives you for leaving and gets ready to welcome you back in the morning.

I got up before the church bell rang. I made coffee on the stove and drank it while standing. My hands felt steady. My heart didn't need proof. I put on the plain dress that lets my body move and doesn't want to be noticed. I left the apartment with the last of the steam still coming out of the cup in the sink.

The city was brand new in the street. Delivery trucks let out a sigh. A street sweeper went by and used a brush to make soft circles on the stones. The woman at the bakery put warm cornetti in a paper bag right away, without making me wait. I ate mine while I was walking, and the sugar dust fell on my wrist like the first snow.

The sign said "Closed," but Libri e Caffè was open. Giovanni saw me through the glass and waved me in by raising his chin. The bell rang like it does in the morning: clear and small.

He said, "You are early."

"That's what you told me to do," I said.

He laughed. "True."

The box of used books next to the counter was full of lives that were ready to be found again. He put another one on a chair. We got down on our knees and started to sort. Covers that had been handled by a lot of people. Spines with exact breaks, like lines on a hand. Margins with the private thoughts of people you don't know.

We talked like people do when their hands are busy and their minds are free. We read the first sentences of our favourite books out loud. We told each other little stories about the people who bought them and the people who sent them back. He said that his mother once put a poem inside a cookbook so that his father would find it when he went to get sugar. He asked me why my grandmother kept pictures in her dictionary, and I told him that meaning and memory went together.

The hours went by like good weather. We stood still for a while just to feel our knees again. We drank some water. He cut an orange with a small knife he kept in a drawer, and we shared it. That bright smell filled the room. We kept on going.

The light in the window changed at noon. He stood up, stretched, and looked at the piles we had made.

"Look," he said. "Good job."

"Yes," I said. "It's better than good."

He put his arms on the counter and leaned against it. Then he unfolded his arms, as if arms aren't meant to be a wall.

He said, "Sophia."

I raised my head.

He said, "There is a kind of peace that comes over a person when they stop fighting with the day. I see it in you."

I felt it then, not as a thought but as a fact in my body. "I see it, too," I said.

He turned the sign to "Open," and the bell rang. The first customer of the afternoon walked in and smiled at the smell of coffee and oranges. The city got ready to be itself again.

He touched his fingers to the table and then to his chest before walking to the counter. It was a small thank-you for the work, the room, and the time we had spent.

He said over his shoulder, "Stay for lunch. There's a panino that will make you think differently about what bread can do."

I laughed. "You always say that."

"It is always true," he said, and then he sat down behind the machine like it was a piano.

The afternoon started like a page. People came and went. The sun moved its square of light around on the floor. The city kept making noise. I felt like I belonged without having to hold on too tightly.

There are days when life doesn't want anything from you. It only asks that you show up, tell the truth, be nice when you can, and be brave when you have to. That day was Rome for me. The city did not owe me anything. It didn't say why. It simply asked for the truth and got it.

We locked the door again when it got dark. He took me to the corner and raised his hand in the same small salute as the night before.

He said, "Tomorrow."

"Tomorrow," I repeated.

I went home with clean hands and tired knees, the kind of tired and clean that makes you sleep without a doubt. I wrote one line before bed.

I didn't rush today, and the city was nice to me.

Then I put in the line that was more important.

My heart did, too.

CHAPTER ELEVEN

The Quiet That Comes Between Pages

Some mornings come like a promise, and some mornings feel like practice. The ones I remember best are the ones that happen in the quiet time before the city wakes up, when the shop smells like coffee and paper and anything is possible again. Giovanni slowly opens the front shutters, as if the light were a delicate thing that needed to be handled carefully. He never hurries. That's one of the things I love most about him.

Our routines are small and very specific. He grinds the beans by hand when he can, and the sound is like a small drumbeat that marks the day. I make the milk, watch the steam rise, and fold it like I'm sorry and offering it. He puts the table by the window so that the light is best for reading. He will sometimes put a piece of junk he found in my notebook. A leaf that has dried. A piece of a ticket. He thinks that stories are in things that are found and in the spaces between sentences.

I used to be afraid that my writing had to be a brilliant arc. It is a slow claim. A line, a paragraph, or a thought that won't leave me alone until I give it form. I wrote for myself and for the peace at first. Then people I didn't know started to read the small things I put online. That was odd. That was nice. They said my words made them feel less alone. I didn't know that was possible. I didn't know that a sentence could do the same thing as a hand on the back of your neck.

Giovanni reads my drafts with the same care that he gives to his clients. No praise that seems fake. No compliments. Just a look and a question that always gets to the truth. He will ask you what this line means to you or why you put it here. The paragraph often changes when I answer. He knows how to tell the truth. He stays calm.

One afternoon, he surprised me by leaving the store to get a small book of poems. He came back with a small, ribboned bundle and a quiet smile. The journal was the same colour as old wine. He put it in front of me like a gift and told me to keep it for the work I would one day let the world read. He didn't say to publish. He didn't have to. He never talks like a man who needs other people to praise him. He talks like a man who is happy with himself.

We don't talk much some afternoons. We do what needs to be done. He puts the returned books in piles. I answer emails and then close the laptop because sometimes the most important work can be done without using my hands. We sit in the doorway with our coffee and watch a dog walk by with the confidence of an animal that knows the street map. In that little homey space, everything feels safe.

Our tenderness is not over the top. It comes in small ways, like when he finds the back of my hand with his thumb while I'm looking for a line, or when he stops in the middle of a sentence to make sure I have time to say what I need to say. One night in the courtyard, he grabs my wrist and pulls me back just before I step in a puddle. He laughs like I've been flirting with disaster. He kisses my knuckles quickly and privately, and the world around us gets smaller so we can fit better inside it.

I'm surprised at how easily we fit together. I don't think I ever let myself think about having a friend like this. He talks about his dad sometimes, telling stories full of chestnuts and river air. Those memories shine in him like a private lantern. He doesn't want me to be someone else. He doesn't close his questions, and when I answer, he listens like someone who is holding something fragile.

We take care of each other. That's not the same as being scared. It is an active and happy attention. After a reading one night, a woman came up to me and said, "Your name made me cry." The part about the train. She hugged me with the weight of a stranger and then walked back into the street, feeling lighter. Giovanni saw the exchange and said, "You were very brave." I didn't think of it as brave, but when he said it, it felt like it was true.

There are deep conversations that don't shock you. We talk about both the little and big kinds of happiness. We talk about the places we still want to go. He wants to write his own book. He says that the shop keeps him honest, but the stories that come out when he is alone with a pen are like a second skin to him. I have read a line or two when he either forgot to close the notebook or gave it to me like a gift. The sentences have a soft quality to them. Sometimes there is anger, a steady frustration with how life makes us make choices.

We walked to the market one Sunday because he wanted to buy anise seeds and a new lemon for a tart he had been thinking about. They knew him, the sellers. They called his name without being polite. He joked with a woman who sells olives, and they fought over how to cook the beans the right way. The arguments were dramatic and full of emotion. He walks through the market like he knows everyone is important.

A kid on a bike took a turn that would have hit my ankle if I hadn't stopped laughing first. The kid smiled like mornings are all about being bad. Giovanni looked at me, and later I tried to name the softness in his eyes in the lines I wrote that night. I don't think there is one big confession in our story. There are smaller promises. You can show devotion in many ways. He shows it by remembering how I like my coffee. He shows me that he cares by reading the part I'm worried about and saying, "That's not bad at all."

In moments like that, I think I see you.

We sit at the table with just one lamp on at night, when the shop is closed and the city is quiet, like it is in old towns. We read to each other. He reads from something that is bright and curved, and the words sound like music. When I read my paragraphs, my voice sometimes shakes. He never lets the tremor change the meaning of the sentence. He waits for me to find the line again, and then he claps his hands together softly, barely touching the paper.

There is also fear. Not the kind that keeps us from going outside. It is more exact. It's scary that two regular people, who are slowly knitting their lives together with small commitments, might not learn how to hold on to their happiness when the future demands everything. We don't talk about it like it's a threat. We talk about how to make mornings matter, what anchors to set up, and how to keep a rhythm so that when decisions come up later, we will already know how to work together.

There is a knowledge of how fragile time is in the spaces between our words. It isn't dark. It is just a better way to see. "You can't hoard mornings," Giovanni says. "You have to make good use of them." He has never been sentimental about pain. He believes that life should be lived to the fullest. He wants to try everything he can because he knows that a lot of life is normal and can't be replaced.

He held my face in his hands, like a surgeon does before making a delicate cut, when I was scared to give my writing away and fail in front of everyone. He said, "It doesn't matter if ten people read this or a thousand. The work will find its rightful owners. Everything else is noise." I can't tell you how much that helped me. The words became something I could say without being afraid.

But the whole world is not one feeling. There are a lot of them. The city calls and changes while we wait. People come and go as customers. People who used to just walk by my store now stop to ask about my classes and volunteer sessions. Because of the life we have chosen, the room stretches in ways we didn't expect. The story we live is louder and softer than any chapter I've ever written.

There are nights when we sleep with our ankles touching, and in the morning, we both reach for the same cup of coffee without looking. He takes my hand, and for a brief, honest moment, there is no future to worry about and no past to hold us back. There is only the steady fact that we are two people who keep coming back.

I am learning how to live a life that doesn't require me to give up myself. Giovanni helps me get better. He is patient when I still trip over some old shape of shame. When I try to give a dramatic speech and end up saying something silly, he laughs right away. When I need the silence to think of the right sentence, he is quiet. He is everything that has taught me how important it is to have normal days.

When I think about what matters now, it's not fireworks or promises that don't take any work. The smell of coffee, the sound of pages turning slowly, and his hand on my back when I step down from the shop counter. It is a small, steady love that doesn't need proof. It only asks that we be there. That's enough for now. That's all there is.

The days that came after each other were like soft paper. The city's pace became my own: slow in the morning and not rushed at night. I started to love how the light in Rome moved. It didn't go in a straight line; instead, it made gestures, stayed on stone, paused on faces, and curled through alleyways like it didn't want to leave.

Giovanni once said that the city breathes differently when it rains. He was correct. The cobblestones sparkled in the morning, and the air smelled like iron and wet leaves. We would open the shutters and let the sun shine in. The smell of espresso wafted out into the street, bringing in our regulars: the old professor who always brought his folded newspaper, the young couple who argued about novels as if the world depended on it, and the woman who never spoke but always smiled when she left a book on the counter, paying exactly what she owed.

I started to write about them. Not their names, but the small things they did every day. How the professor kept reading about wars that were long over. How the woman put wildflowers in the pages of the books she bought. How Giovanni always found a way to be with them, whether it was with a story, a joke, or silence.

When I wrote about them, I noticed more and saw more. After years of routine, the world became bright again. Words were how I touched it.

When the store was quiet in the afternoons, Giovanni and I would sit on the steps outside and drink coffee that had gone cold. The sound of church bells rang out over the rooftops, and kids laughed in the street. We talked about nothing at times. Sometimes, about everything.

"I used to think happiness was a place to go," I said one afternoon. "Something you got for working hard enough."

He smiled without looking at me. "And now?"

"Now I see it," I said. "Of staying."

He nodded his head. "Maybe it's both. You have to go a long way to learn how to stay still."

After that, we sat still and watched a boy chase a pigeon down the street. His laughter shot up like a flare. Giovanni turned his head and said, "That's what happiness sounds like when no one is listening."

I liked the evenings in the store the most. The light got thinner, and the books turned gold. Giovanni would hum, always something he half-remembered, like a song his mother used to sing. I learned to tell it apart by its breaks more than its notes. He would hum and I would write, and in those moments, everything seemed to be in its right place.

Rome was covered in fog when winter came. The windows also fogged up, and when no one was looking, I drew little hearts and shapes on the glass. Giovanni caught me once and raised an eyebrow.

"An artist now?"

"Only in condensation," I said.

He laughed. "The best kind. It goes away before it can make you feel bad."

He had that kind of humour: light but sharp, teasing without being mean. It was one of the reasons I could breathe next to him without feeling small.

We started a new tradition as the days got shorter. Every Thursday night, after the store closed, we would cook together in the small kitchen at the back of the store. It wasn't much—just a stove, a counter, and an old wooden table. But it was ours. I would cut up the vegetables while he made the sauce. He cooked slowly, carefully, and without wasting anything, just like he talked.

He once said to me, "You put too much salt in the soup."

"I like flavour," I said.

"And I like balance," he said as he added water.

We came to an agreement. That became our beat as well.

Those dinners turned into big meals. We didn't have anything fancy—just pasta, bread, olives, and a glass of red wine to share—but cooking together made time seem to stretch. We talked about the past sometimes. Sometimes about what's to come.

He once told me that he never thought he would stay in Rome for this long. "I thought I would travel the world," he said as he wiped his hands on a towel. "But the city made me different. Or maybe I let it happen.

"Do you wish you hadn't stayed?" I asked.

He thought about it for a while, then shook his head. "No. I believe I found the right kind of stillness."

I didn't tell him that I thought he was the stillness that lets other people breathe.

I sat alone at the table that night, the smell of garlic still in the air and the sound of the city coming through the walls. I opened my diary and wrote:

There are times when we meet people who don't move us forward or backward but deeper.

Weeks went by. People from places I'd never been read my blog. People sent me small notes saying that my words gave them the strength to try again, forgive someone, leave, or stay. Giovanni printed some of them out and put them up behind the counter. He said they were proof that stories have their own places.

One night, while I was putting books on the shelf, he quietly said, "You've become a part of this place."

I looked at him and didn't know what to say.

"I mean it," he said again. "The customers want you. They believe in your taste. You make something come to life here. Perhaps it's because you see people."

His words stuck with me. For years, I felt like I was invisible, living behind my own reflection. It was like light touching water after years of being in the dark.

That night, as I walked home through the cool, smoky air, I thought about how much Rome had changed me, or maybe how much it had let me change myself. I didn't look for a way out anymore. I looked for presence. I didn't think about what I hadn't done anymore; instead, I thought about what I'd seen, what I'd done, and what I'd shared.

Giovanni once said that everyone has a book inside them. I used to think he meant that in a figurative way. But now I got it. You don't write the story. You live it, line by line, until it becomes your voice.

Giovanni found me drawing the storefront on a piece of paper one afternoon as spring was slowly coming back to the city. He smiled and looked over my shoulder.

"Are you planning to make changes?" he asked.

I said, "Just remembering. In case things change again."

He stopped, and for the first time in a long time, I saw something move across his face—a shadow that wasn't there before.

For a moment, I wondered if he was hiding a worry of his own.

It left a mark, but it was gone almost as soon as it came.

He said softly, "Change is good. Even when it doesn't feel like it."

I didn't ask him what he meant. Sometimes, silence should be respected.

That night, as we were cleaning up, the smell of old paper and coffee was stronger than usual. The first stars were starting to show up in the cool air outside. Giovanni turned off the lights one by one, walking through the store like he was trying to remember where everything was.

He turned to me as he reached the door and said, "Don't stop writing. Even when it hurts. Especially at that time."

It wasn't goodbye yet, but the words settled in me like a seed pressed into the ground.

I saw him walk down the street, and his shadow disappeared into the light of the streetlights. It was a normal night, but it also felt fragile, like something had just changed but hadn't yet shown its shape.

I stood there for a long time after he left, my hand on the glass door, feeling the echo of his words in my chest.

The silence between the pages had changed again.

CHAPTER TWELVE

The Old Rough Road

We sat on a bench in the park in the late afternoon and watched the fountain throw little silver knives into the air. The kids screamed when the water got them. Above us, the leaves made a noise that made us feel uneasy. None of it got to me. Memory has its own space. It was loud today. I wasn't ready for what surfaced, but the past rarely waits for permission.

I shut my eyes and then opened them again. The past didn't wait for an invitation. It moved forward like a family member who knows your door code.

I was twenty-three years old and wearing a lace dress that was too tight at the waist. The church smelled like lilies and floor cleaner. People said I looked beautiful. I felt like someone had cut out a picture and put it in the wrong place. As I walked down the aisle, my stomach hurt like it was full of pins. I told myself it was just nerves. I thought love would be enough. The promise seemed big enough to cover everything. I said yes like a swimmer who was holding her breath.

There were signs even back then. I saw them and called them by a different name.

The week before the wedding, my boss, a nice man everyone called Boss, pulled me aside at work. We stood by the copy machine while it warmed up. He rubbed his jaw and gave me a worried look.

"You light up a room," he said. "You don't hide. I don't get how a controlling man fits that light."

I laughed because it was easier than crying. "I don't feel like he's controlling me," I said. "He is trying." It is a stage.

Lajo, a friend of mine, met me for coffee and asked what I was thinking. He said, "Don't marry fear. You can do better." I made a joke and changed the subject. Some part of me knew I was lying to both of us.

He could be charming when he wanted to be. That was one part of it. He could sell a dry riverbed to a town that needed water. He told the story of his childhood with such passion on our second date that people at a nearby table leaned in to listen. When I met him, he wasn't talking to his sister. He held grudges like trophies. He wore his anger like a nice coat. I told myself that it was the weather he had grown up in. I told myself I would be the spring.

The marriage quickly got tighter around me. The first few weeks were easy. Then the voice he used with other people started to come to me. It got sharper when things didn't go his way. It hurt when dinner was twenty minutes late or the house didn't look right. Words hurt before hands do. They leave colours that no one else can see.

Our house got used to the sound of careful steps. I learned what kinds of breaths were okay. I found out that a "hello" on my phone could be an accusation. I learned that being quiet doesn't mean being at peace. When someone is silent, they are holding their breath so that no one can hear them.

Some moments never go away. They wait in a corner.

He threw up his hands one night at a gas station and said, "Why am I always driving you? I pay for the gas. I pick you up. What do you even do?"

"I'll pay," I said. My hand shook when I reached for my wallet.

He pulled my bag off my shoulder and threw it out the door. He left in his car. I stood there with the smell of gas in my hair and my heart pounding in my chest.

Fifteen minutes later, a coworker saw me walking along the side of the road and stopped.

"This isn't safe," he said, and he meant more than just the road.

He came home late one night and demanded food. I made dinner and put the plate down. He pushed it away with two fingers. "Forget it. I'm not hungry," he said, and then he locked the kitchen and put the key in his pocket. He locked the bedroom the next day while he took a shower. He read my texts and asked me questions I couldn't answer because they weren't about the truth.

In my mind, I kept moving the target. *If I only change this. If I just give that a shot. If I talk less. If I can learn to look around corners.* It's amazing how small you can get and still be seen as too big.

When he hit me for the first time, light burst behind my eyes like someone had shaken the stars loose. He cried after that. He got some flowers. He put his head in my lap and said he was stressed. He promised it would never happen again. I wanted to believe him because if I did, I wouldn't have to blow up the life I had just built. It happened again.

That day, when he said my parents would come to get my body if I tried to leave, something inside me broke that had never broken before. The fear of staying finally became stronger than the fear of leaving. I think everyone who leaves knows this exact amount. No one else can do the weighing for you.

I packed without talking. I folded shirts like I was saying sorry to them. The zipper on the suitcase sounded like a wire being pulled through the house. I moved slowly but carefully. I put the papers I needed in a file. I put money in my shoe. The cap on the toothpaste rolled under the cabinet because my hands were shaking so much. I didn't go after it.

The latch on the door felt loud enough to wake up the street when I closed it. I pushed the suitcase to the car and didn't look at the windows. I cried and drove until I couldn't see. I stopped at a gas station and cried some more while the air compressor let out a tired sigh. A woman in a red jacket knocked on the glass and gave me napkins. She didn't say anything. She didn't have to.

The divorce was bad. He was late to meetings, so I would feel small in my own chair. He threw words around the room like coins that were very sharp. He tried to get my friends to pick. Some did not. A few did. Courtrooms don't smell like justice. They smell like coffee and old carpet. I kept coming back. I signed everything that needed to be signed. Every time someone called my name, I put both feet on the floor. The judge said two sentences, and my life changed in ways that felt like miles.

I lived alone for the first time in a small apartment with a door that stuck in the summer. The rooms felt empty and real. I had a pan and two bowls. I slept on a mattress on the floor because the bed frame was still in a box, and I couldn't put it together without shaking. At first, the quiet hurt. It hurt because it belonged to me.

Then the pain changed. I could hear the refrigerator breathing. I heard rain on the roof, and no one said it was a problem. Every morning, sunlight made a thin, bright line on the floor, and I learned to put my foot in it. I made tea and drank it all. I bought a plant and took care of it. I laughed at a show and didn't cover my mouth. I put up a picture of myself when I was twenty and told her I was sorry for not listening sooner.

Friends helped me out in small ways. One person came with a toolbox and put the bed together. She put her extra key in my hand and said, "Come over whenever you want. Don't knock." One person sat on the kitchen floor with me and ate takeout straight from the paper box while we took turns holding the fork. Sometimes, help is silent. It can look like someone is sitting on your floor to remind you that you have a body.

I owe my life to therapy. I held my bag close to my chest like a life vest during the first session. I talked quickly to get rid of the shame. My therapist had calm eyes and shoes that were good for walking a long way.

She said, "You are not broken. It's not your fault what happened to you."

I didn't believe her. It takes time to believe. There was a citrus and paper smell in her office. I went there every week and learned how to sit with myself without being afraid of what would happen. I learned that I had put a lot of energy into controlling someone else's weather. I learned to look at the sky to see what the weather will be like.

A few months later, she asked me if I would think about joining a group. I said no, but I still sat in a circle. Chairs that fold up. Water in plastic cups. A smooth handoff of tissues, like in a relay race. For the first hour, I just looked at a spot on the floor where the linoleum had been fixed. Then, a woman with a bird tattoo on her wrist said, "He asked me who I thought I was." A woman with perfect nails said, "He unplugged my alarm so I would be late." A man with careful hair said, "He told me no one else would love me." The stories were all different. They were known. Shame is a bully who doesn't like the sun. We both turned on the light.

I started to take back small areas. I picked the blue mug because I thought it looked good in my hand. I wore a red dress to the store for no reason at all. In the summer, I didn't wear socks to bed. I learned how to make a meal I wanted and ate it with both of my elbows on the table. It seems silly to write down progress, but you need it to stay alive.

When I went out to dinner alone for the first time, the waiter asked, "Are you expecting anyone?" and I said, "Just me." He then gave me a table by the window and didn't rush me. I took my time eating. I saw a couple fight over olives. I watched a kid drop a fork with the satisfaction of a scientist and then do it again. I didn't check my phone once during the meal. The sky hadn't changed when I walked home, and I felt taller.

•‚Ä¢●•‚Ä¢

I didn't talk much about the marriage. Putting the words together made them feel heavy. I put them in a drawer in my chest. I opened the drawer a little bit at a time. One night, I took the whole drawer out and put it on the table in front of Giovanni.

We were by the Tiber on the stone wall. The river moved like a big animal that was trying to look slow. The last light touched the water and then went away. I had been too quiet for too long. He didn't push. He has never been the kind of person who thinks that being patient means being lazy.

I said, "I have to tell you something." The words stuck together. I carefully pulled them apart.

"Don't rush," he said. He looked at my face the whole time. He didn't fill the space with his own story.

I told him. Not everything. That's enough. I told him about the kitchen, the gas station, and the day I put money in my shoe. I told him about the first slap and how sorry I was after. I told him that shame is like a wet coat and fear is like a room with no doors. I told him the line that finally broke the spell and the sound the zipper on the suitcase made. I told him that when the judge said my name, something inside me stood up. Words that had been like stones in my mouth turned into water.

My hands were shaking when I was done. I pressed them together and waited for him to tell me what to do or feel sorry for me. He didn't.

He said, "Pain can change you without owning you." He spoke in a steady voice. "It can carve out a space for light to come in."

He didn't reach for me right away. He let what I said float away in the air. After that, he put his hand on mine. Warm. Normal. The kind of touch that doesn't try to change anything. It made me remember that I had a body.

We saw the river go under the bridge. A boy with a paper airplane ran by and almost fell. Someone up there played a guitar. The city kept doing what it does. He spoke again when it was almost dark.

"You've already done the hardest part," he said. "You went."

I said, "Some days, I still feel like I'm there."

"That's not you," he said. "That's the echo. You don't get to choose your life based on echoes."

I let that line stay in me. It found a chair and put its feet on it.

After that night, I started volunteering at the community centre. Helping other people made me feel useful again. I picked easy things to do. Putting books on top of each other. Giving out pencils. Reading next to a boy who had lost his place and needed to find it without being asked why. There was a smell of paper and hope in the room. I went back because I liked who I was when I was there.

Travel came back slowly. First short trips. A train to a town with one square and three coffee shops. A bus ride to a hill with olive trees and a view that took my breath away. Every time, I brought myself home with very little. Every little trip showed me that I could leave and come back without breaking.

I learned more about what it felt like to be steady on the inside the more I moved. It didn't feel like standing still. I felt like I knew where my feet were as I took the next step.

Even as I got better, a feeling I had been hiding from myself began to wake up like a bird behind a curtain. I wanted to have a baby. When the idea hit me, it shocked me. I kept telling myself I was too old, too late, too much, or not enough. The rules in my head were made up by a fear that I didn't know who I was.

I said it out loud one day while sitting on a bench like this one.

"I want to be a mom," I said. The words shook. I did not give them back.

Giovanni didn't move. He looked at me like he looked at a page that was almost done. He said, "It's not too late. You've already done the impossible." He didn't promise me anything he couldn't keep. He gave faith, which is not the same as a promise. "You can walk through faith one step at a time."

We sat there until the light went behind the buildings and the air made my arms feel cool. My scars didn't own me. I owned them. I looked at him and felt the strange calm that comes when your mind and body are finally in sync.

I said, "Thank you. For staying. For seeing me."

"You were strong," he said. "I just held the lantern."

The city had put on its evening face when we stood up. We took our time getting home. People walked by with their bags of bread and tired voices. A woman in a red coat crossed the street slowly. I watched how she walked, as if she had made up her mind to keep going.

I opened my notebook when I got back to my apartment. The cover was bent. There was coffee on the first page. I wrote in a clear way. Not a talk. A record. I stopped writing after I said what I could. The next night, I wrote again. I didn't break when I told the truth. It opened up space for a different sound inside me. At first, it was small. Then it was a voice.

There were problems. Of course, there were. The road to healing isn't straight. I would wake up in the middle of the night and forget what life I was in. A slammed door would sometimes let the old air back in. I would sometimes stand in the shower and let the water run until it got cold because I wanted to feel something that made sense.

I practiced three things on those days. I said one good thing I could see. The plant. The spoon. The square of the sun on the wall. I said something true to myself. *You are safe right now.* I did one small thing to start the day. Put two towels in half. Clean the table. Put an egg in boiling water. The little things made a knot in the rope so I could hold on.

The old, bumpy road didn't go away. I learned how to walk it without tripping over the same rocks. I learned how to turn my face away from the ditch. I learned where the ground changed and how to walk lightly.

Years later, when I was sitting on this bench with Giovanni and the fountain was throwing light and kids into the air, I realized I wasn't telling a sad story. I was telling the truth. The truth was sad and full of hope. It had fear and the choice to go anyway. The girl in the lace dress and the woman who packed her own car were both in it. It had the part of me that thought love meant getting smaller and the part that knows love is the opposite.

We got up to leave. The sun had gone behind the buildings, leaving the leaves with silver edges. As he locked his bike, a man whistled. While she was on the phone, a dog leaned against her leg. In the best way, the world looked normal again.

"Gelato," Giovanni said. His voice brought the light back.

I said, "Two scoops. Two scoops is dinner."

He laughed, and we walked toward the cones that smelled like chestnuts. I was both tired and wide awake at the same time. I felt like someone who had learned to carry what she could and leave behind what she couldn't. I felt like I was finally wearing a coat that fit me.

We crossed the bridge on the way home, and the river looked like a long piece of dark silk. Years ago, I remembered the woman in the red jacket giving me napkins through the glass. I wanted to find her and tell her how the story ended. I wish I could have given my past self a stack of napkins and told her to keep going. There is more.

Giovanni touched the door of my building and then stepped back so I could open it. That was nice of him to do. I liked that he let me go first. I liked that he didn't call it chivalry. He said it was respect.

Because I had wiped the counter with half a lemon and some salt that morning, the room smelled like lemons. I put two bowls on the table and divided the gelato in a way that seemed fair. He gets pistachio. For me, hazelnut. We didn't talk while we ate. The silence wasn't heavy. It was full. The kind that comes with two chairs and a table.

He dried the bowls after I washed them. That night, we didn't talk about the past again. We didn't have to. It was already in the room. It was a stone that kept the table leg steady when the floor was uneven.

I stood at the window and watched the street calm down after he left. A man pulled a suitcase that wouldn't budge over the stones. A cat sat under the streetlight and thought about what it would do next. A piano somewhere played the same four notes over and over until they turned into a song.

I put my hand on the cool glass. The old, bumpy road was behind me and in me. That's how roads work. You take them. You find out how they bend. You find out which way to turn to get back to yourself.

I went to bed and slept like a field does after it rains. Not quite right. That's enough.

CHAPTER THIRTEEN

Finding My Voice

The first mornings after, the park bench was different. The light came in more slowly. The air felt softer, like the world had decided not to rush me anymore. My small apartment looked the same, but I felt like I was seeing it for the first time. The kitchen clock's soft ticking, the refrigerator's hum, and the shuffle of footsteps in the courtyard below were all new sounds. There was no more silence. It was an empty space.

I started making coffee the way Giovanni had taught me, letting the smell fill the room before I poured the first drop. I would sit by the window with a notebook and look at the blank page. I wasn't writing yet. The page didn't blame me anymore. It stayed still.

There were days when the pain still came. I would wake up in the middle of the night and feel the familiar pressure in my chest, which was a quiet reminder of what I had lost. But I was learning how to face it without being afraid. I realized that grief was no longer an intruder. It had become a part of my heart's furniture.

I walked to the café where Giovanni first gave me *Jane Eyre* one afternoon. The bell over the door still rang the same little bell. The shelves still had their uneven rows of books, and Isabella was behind the counter, laughing with a student about a word that was said wrong. She smiled when she saw me. "You are back," she said plainly. I nodded. It was enough.

I sat down at the table by the window, the same one where I had read *Pride and Prejudice*, and opened my notebook. The first line came in a soft voice: *Today, I will start over*. It was a short sentence, but it meant a lot to me because of all the work I had done to get there. I kept writing. Nothing is perfect. Not poetic at all. Only bits of the truth. The dust sparkled in the morning light. How coffee had started to taste like hope again.

I was still at the café when Giovanni came by later that day. My notebook was open next to an empty cup. He put a new book by Rilke on the table and looked at me with a question in his eyes. I turned the notebook around to face him. He read a few lines and then carefully closed it.

He said, "You are starting to sound like yourself again."

I smiled. "I don't know who that is yet."

He said, "Then keep writing until you find her," and for the first time in years, I believed him.

After his shift on Tuesdays, we started to meet. He would read a part of a book sometimes, and other times we would talk about the people who came and went through the café doors. He paid attention to the smallest things, like how someone held a cup or how someone paused before opening a book. He would say, "Everyone is telling a story. Most people don't even know it."

I started to watch that way, too. The young woman who read Neruda with her lips moving silently and had paint under her nails. The old man came every morning at eight, ordered one espresso, and left a newspaper perfectly folded on the chair. The city itself started to talk again, but not with words. I wrote about each one of them.

Weeks went by, and something soft started to grow. I was less afraid of the page. I filled up one notebook, then another. I wrote about how the rain sounded against the shutters and how Roman light turned buildings into gold before nightfall. I wrote about how Giovanni's laugh filled every corner of the room.

After I read him a few paragraphs one night, he leaned back in his chair and said, "You should share this."

"With whom?" I asked.

He said, "With anyone who needs to hear it."

I was scared of the idea. Writing had been a private thing, like prayer. But his eyes were calm and kind. So I did. I started a small online column. I named it The Quiet Hours. I wrote short pieces about bravery, learning to stay, and how being alone can feel heavy and light. I didn't think anyone would read them. But messages started to show up.

Your words were like a mirror.

Thanks for saying what I couldn't.

I believed I was the only one.

Every message felt like a hand reaching out from the dark. It felt like the pain I had been carrying was now being used for something bigger than me. When I told Giovanni, he smiled. "Look," he said. "You gave your silence a reason."

As the weeks turned into months, my days started to fill up again. I worked part-time at a library nearby, where I could hear the soft sound of pages turning. I met people who came for peace and quiet but stayed to talk. I volunteered at a small writing group on Saturdays. We sat in a circle and wrote about things that scared us. A woman wrote about how she lost her husband. A man wrote about how he wasn't seen. We read out loud, and sometimes we cried. But each time, the room felt lighter.

My apartment started to change at home. Plants I had ignored for years began to grow again. I hung up pictures from my trips and framed a postcard Giovanni had sent me that said, "Every morning we are born again."

One morning, the light coming through the window was so soft that I stopped making coffee to watch it. The room smelled warm and like paper. I realized I was no longer surviving. I was alive.

Giovanni suggested a trip that spring. He said, "You've been writing about Rome for too long. Let the world remind you that it is bigger than one city."

We took a train to Florence. It was a slow ride, the kind that lets you think. There were fields of green and gold rolling by outside. Giovanni read from a book of Italian poems out loud. His voice was low and steady. I leaned my head against the glass and let the words and movement take me.

The air in Florence smelled like rain and old stone. Places can sound the same even when they are on different continents. Florence calmed me like Jos used to do at dusk, when the sky turned pale blue and the air felt like a song. Rome had always had the same restless pulse as Lagos, alive, never stopping, and never sleeping. But standing by the Arno, I felt the peace my soul had been looking for for years.

We walked along the Arno and saw how the light danced on the water. We sat on the steps by the bridge at sunset and listened to a violinist play. The notes floated across the water, soft and shaking.

Giovanni said, "I used to think music was what we hear. Now I think it's what moves between us when we listen."

I couldn't get his words out of my mind. The city was bright and warm all around us. That night, in the small hotel room, I wrote about how sound and silence could live together without fighting.

We went from Florence to the Amalfi Coast. The roads twisted like ribbons through cliffs and lemon trees. The sea below changed from turquoise to deep blue. It was calm and went on forever. We stayed in a guesthouse in a small village with whitewashed walls and windows that opened to the water. Every morning, I woke up to the smell of salt and the sun.

Some places stick with you not because of where they are, but because they remind you of something inside you.

Rome had the same restless heartbeat as Lagos for me: loud, flawed, full of survival and unspoken strength. Florence calmed me down like Jos used to do in the early evenings, when the sky turned blue and quiet, and the world felt soft.

Amalfi made me believe in light again, just like when I stood by the Erin-Ijesha Waterfalls back home and felt the weight of the world lift as the water roared over the rocks, reminding me that even broken things could be washed clean.

I realized that I wasn't just going through cities; something inside me was moving, too.

Giovanni had a small basket with figs and cheese. We sat quietly, like we were praying. "You know," he finally said, "you are not the same woman who came into the café that first day."

I said, "I feel different. Somehow lighter. But I'm worried it will go away."

"It won't," he said. "Change doesn't go away when life gets quiet. It turns into the calm."

I looked out at the horizon. There was no line between the sea and the sky. "Do you really think that?"

He nodded. "I've seen you put yourself back together. You are proof that we start over many times in our lives."

I smiled. "You make it sound easy."

He said, "It's not easy. It is needed."

I wrote for hours that night while cicadas softly hummed. Words flowed like water, steady and sure. I wrote about how endings can look like beginnings, how hard it is to stay open, and how a small act of kindness can change the course of a day.

When I was done, I left the notebook on the table open. The wind blew the pages up, and I could see them move like the words were breathing.

I kept writing when I got back to Rome. My audience grew, but it was never about the numbers. It was all about making connections. At the café, I would sometimes see people who knew me. People would thank me for something I had written, and I would tell them that it was their own bravery that made it happen.

One night, I saw Giovanni sitting at our usual table and reading a letter. He looked up when I got close. "From our old friend," he said. "He wrote to say that he still finds joy in little things, even after losing."

I nodded. "That sounds familiar."

He grinned. "Because you taught him that."

After that, we sat in silence, the kind of silence that makes you feel like you understand. People were laughing and walking around in the city outside. A bell rang somewhere. I could feel the sound in my chest, steady and calm.

"Do you ever wonder what will happen next?" I asked him.

He looked at me for a long time before he spoke. "Every day," he said. "But not with fear. With interest."

While I was walking home, I thought about that. The rain made the streets shiny and smooth, and the light bounced off of them in soft pools. For the first time, the future didn't seem like something to be afraid of. It felt like a path I was ready to take.

I opened my notebook again that night. I wrote about the train rides, the laughter, the café tables, and the quiet conversations that had brought me here. I wrote about how I thought I had lost my voice. I wrote about Giovanni and how he had become the mirror that helped me see myself.

I had never felt so calm before when I closed the notebook. It wasn't a quiet that comes from being alone. It was the quiet.

I went to the balcony and looked out at the city. The moon was low in the sky over the rooftops. Someone played a guitar softly and shakily somewhere below. The sound floated up like a memory.

At that moment, I learned something simple and true: healing doesn't come like the sun rising. It comes in flashes, when you least expect it, and in the quiet act of choosing life again.

I sent one of my stories to a small literary magazine that had turned me down before the next morning. I didn't do it to get approval. I did it to honour the part of me that had been too scared to try before.

The city felt alive under my feet as I walked away from the post office. There was a lot of blue sky above. I remembered what Giovanni said: "Keep writing until you find her."

I smiled to myself. I was still looking, but for the first time in years, I liked who I was becoming.

I felt like the city was whispering back to me, "You are already found" when the wind brushed my cheek, warm and steady.

Giovanni mentioned Marrakech one evening as we stood on the balcony, the city stretched out below us. He didn't make it sound like a plan, only a place he had once loved for its open roofs and warm nights, a city that asked nothing of you but attention. I didn't answer him then. But later, as the wind moved through the streets, I realized the idea had stayed with me.

CHAPTER FOURTEEN

A Surprise Love in Marrakech

That night, the air in Marrakech felt alive. It was warm and heavy with spices and jasmine, and it wrapped around us as if the city was listening. The lanterns swung softly in the wind, and their golden light caught the edges of our faces. The sound of the market rose and fell from below. There was laughter, the soft music of strangers, and the world kept going on while we sat apart from it.

Giovanni was quiet next to me. He had been for a while. We had been talking about nothing and everything, like books, memory, and how sometimes silence speaks louder than words. I turned to him, ready to tease him for falling asleep again, but the look in his eyes stopped me.

He wasn't lost in thought. He was gathering courage.

Finally, he said in a low, almost careful voice, "I have something to tell you."

My heart changed. "What is it?"

He looked down for a second and ran one finger around the edge of his glass. The light from the lamp touched his hand, and for a moment, I saw the tremor there. It wasn't fear; it was feeling held too long.

He said, "I love you." The words fell softly, but they were heavy with years. I had thought for years that intimacy was a power play and that love was a door with a lock on his side of the handle. It now felt like a room with the window open and the light on. There was nothing to gain or prove with him. We both knew what we were doing when we made the choice.

At first, I didn't say anything. I could feel the air catch and the space between us get smaller. His eyes stayed on mine, steady and waiting. I thought about every moment that had led us to this point, every conversation that felt like a confession, and every laugh that felt like a promise we were too scared to name.

He kept going quietly. "I have for a long time. I just didn't want to put what we already had at risk."

My throat hurt. For a heartbeat, I forgot how to take a breath. And then, without even thinking about it, I said, "I love you, too."

The words came out like breath: fragile but real.

Then something changed. The world below us, the music, the heat, and the pulse of life kept moving, but for us, time seemed to stop. He took my hand and didn't hurry. His fingers found mine, and I felt something inside me let go, as if my body had been holding its breath for years.

I met him halfway when he leaned in.

There was no rush for the first kiss. It was a discovery. His mouth touched mine lightly, as if he were asking a question. The air between us got thicker and more meaningful. I could feel my heart beating against my ribs so hard that I thought he could hear it. I remember the mint tea on his breath, the faint salt on his skin, and the warmth that spread through me like the morning sun finding the edge of a curtain.

He pulled back for a moment to look at my face. "Are you sure?" he said in a low voice.

I nodded. "I've never been more sure."

We didn't move fast. The night gave us time to open up. The city around us faded into shadows and sounds. In the distance, a call to prayer could be heard, and footsteps faded away in the narrow alleys. He moved his hand to my face and traced the line of my jaw and the curve of my mouth. Every touch felt both new and familiar, like we had been here before in a different life.

The air inside the small villa was warm and sweet with the smell of orange blossom. The only light came from the window, where a pale moon was stretching across the sheets. Giovanni's shirt brushed against my arm, and his breath matched mine. We talked without words, making small, human sounds that said everything words couldn't.

When his lips touched my neck, I felt the world tilt. His hands moved carefully, not hungrily, as if he were learning a language we both already knew. Every move had a meaning, such as love, respect, or awe. The space between us was full of life. My body shook, not because I was scared but because I realized that love could be this soft, this safe, and this full.

When we finally got together, it wasn't an escape; it was a return. The kind of closeness that makes the lines between memory and skin disappear. He said my name in a whisper, and I felt it all over. It wasn't perfect, but that made it beautiful. I wouldn't have noticed if the world outside had ended.

Afterward, we lay still, our breaths slowly coming back together. He put his hand on my heart as if to make sure it was still beating. The light from the lantern outside flickered across the wall like water.

He looked at me with soft, curious eyes. "You feel like home," he said.

I smiled, and a tear fell on my lip. I whispered back, "You've always been home."

After that, we didn't talk. We didn't have to. The city was quiet now. It felt like the air was listening. I fell asleep with his arm around me, the smell of his skin and jasmine in my hair, and the sound of the desert wind coming in through the open window.

I didn't feel haunted by the past for the first time in a long time.

For the first time, I felt like I fit in.

I woke up before dawn. The air in the room was still warm and smelled like him: citrus, salt, and sleep. The city had not yet woken up outside. The call to prayer was only a soft murmur that came through the window, rising and falling like a soft breath.

I lay there for a long time and watched him. Giovanni was lying on his side with his face toward me and his hair falling across his forehead. He looked younger in the dim light, almost like a boy. It was peaceful in a way that made my heart ache.

I wanted to touch his face, but I didn't. I just watched him take a breath.

It felt like something holy the night before. Not because it was perfect—because it wasn't—but because it was honest. Every pause, every sigh, and every word we said to each other had been real. There were no more masks or stories to hide behind. It was just two people meeting in the middle of life and deciding not to run away.

The sheets were wrapped around us, and they felt good against my skin. My body still remembered how heavy his hands were, how he had traced the small scar near my shoulder without saying anything, and how he had looked at me as if I were becoming, not broken.

For a long time, I thought that intimacy was a way to get power. That love had rules, conditions, and a cost. But what happened last night changed that truth. Giovanni hadn't tried to own me. He had just been there, patient, kind, and not afraid to see me.

The sky outside started to get brighter. I got out of bed quietly and wrapped the sheet around me as I walked to the balcony. The city below looked like a watercolour painting, with the first pale gold of morning on the rooftops. The smell of cardamom rose into the air as smoke from the early cooking fires curled up. A rooster crowed somewhere.

I leaned on the railing and let the dawn come. The stone was cool against my arms. It was like being at the edge of something big and unknown. My heart was steady, but my body shook, as if it remembered being seen too clearly.

I heard the bed creak behind me. Then his voice, which was low and rough from sleep.

He said softly, "You disappeared."

I turned around. He sat up, the sheet falling off his chest, and his hair was a mess. Seeing him, unguarded and human, made me smile.

"I didn't want to wake you up," I said.

"You didn't," he said quietly. He stretched and then stood next to me. The air between us was warm again, the kind that doesn't need to be named.

We stood there together and watched the sun rise over the city.

Giovanni reached for my hand, and his fingers found mine as if they had always known where to go. He said quietly, "I used to think love had to be loud. Great. Lots of gestures. But this…" He pointed to the waking city and us. "This seems true."

"Yes, it does," I said.

He looked at me with searching eyes and a soft voice. "Do you wish you hadn't done it?"

I shook my head. "No. I think I've been waiting for this for a long time."

He let out a breath that sounded like both relief and surprise. Then he kissed my forehead and leaned in. "Then I have too."

The light got brighter and spilled over the rooftops, making the room look like it was made of gold. He made coffee and moved around the small kitchen like someone who had done it a thousand times before. I stood in the doorway and watched him hum to himself and the steam rise around him.

Our fingers touched when he gave me the cup. It was a small thing, but it felt huge. The start of something that would grow.

We sat on the balcony and drank without talking. The city below us woke up completely. We heard voices, carts, laughter, and the sound of water being poured into metal basins. Life went on.

Giovanni looked at me with a thoughtful look on his face. He said, "You know, every story I've ever loved starts with someone making the choice to stay."

I held his gaze. "Then this could be our start."

He nodded slowly. "Maybe it is."

After that, the day went by quietly. As we walked through the Medina, our hands brushed against each other and our steps fell into a rhythm. The world around me seemed louder and brighter, but I felt calm inside, which I hadn't felt before.

Things had changed. Not just between us but also inside of me. The walls I had built out of fear had become less strong. I wasn't looking for forever. I was learning how to be here, in this moment, with this man and this life that kept surprising me.

When we got back to the villa that night, he lit one of the lanterns and put it on the table. The flame shook against the glass. He looked at me the same way he had on the roof: steady and full of quiet love.

We didn't talk. We didn't have to. The light between us said what it needed to.

And deep down, I knew this was what it meant to be found.

The days after that night went by as if they were already known. The city moved around us in waves. The markets spilled colour onto the streets, and at dusk, the sound of prayer filled the air. The heat and light moved slowly.

We quietly fit ourselves into that rhythm.

Every morning, Giovanni would get up before me and walk to the corner stall where an old man sold bread that was still warm from the oven. He always came back with two loaves of bread wrapped in paper that were still steaming and a small bunch of mint. He would give me the mint and say, "For the tea and for luck."

We ate bread and figs and drank thick coffee that came from a metal pot that never stopped whistling on the terrace. He would read a part of a book, or we would talk about nothing. We said everything without saying a word, just a look, a smile, or a touch on the wrist.

The world outside us was still loud, but between us it was quiet, the kind of quiet that makes you feel full.

He traded at the market in his rough Arabic with a hint of Italian, and he laughed when he didn't get what he wanted. The sellers liked him for it. He always paid too much but acted like he didn't. I walked a few steps behind him, quietly admiring him in a way that only comes after years of seeing someone's soul.

He bought me a silver bracelet from a woman whose hands were covered in henna. He said, "A circle has no end" as he slid it onto my wrist. "At this moment."

I smiled. "Then we should not break it."

We spent the afternoons walking through the old gardens, where orange trees were full of fruit. He had a small camera with him and took pictures of everything: like light coming through the lattice, a child chasing a bird, and my hair blowing in the wind. I made fun of him for taking too many pictures. He said, "We forget. I gather things that I don't want to lose."

We went back to the villa at night. The walls kept the warmth of the day, and the city quieted down to the sound of drums in the distance. We lay on the roof and looked up at a sky full of stars that looked like they were close enough to touch. He told me stories that didn't need to be believed, just felt.

"Once," he said, "a boy in Rome found a broken typewriter and wrote his way out of fear."

"You," I said.

He smiled. "Maybe. Or maybe it was someone else who needed to know that words can still make things happen."

We didn't hurry through the days. They gently stretched and folded into each other. The world seemed to go around us, not through us.

When it was time to leave Marrakech, the morning came without any fuss. We took our time packing. Giovanni put the mint sprigs in paper and put them in my bag. He said, "For home."

The sky was pale and tired at the airport. As we waited to board, I watched him lean back with his eyes half-closed, looking both calm and far away. I thought about whether he was thinking what I was: that leaving doesn't change what is real. It just wants you to carry it in a different way.

He reached for my hand again on the plane. We didn't say much. The engines' hum filled the space where words could have been. His thumb made steady circles on my palm, which made me feel grounded.

The air was cooler and the light was softer when we got to Rome. The city welcomed us like an old friend who had seen too much but still smiled when you got there.

Everything in the apartment was the same: the books on the table, the half-empty bottle of olive oil, and the scarf hanging over the chair. But nothing was the same. There was something new in the air. A tenderness that couldn't be hidden.

While I unpacked, Giovanni made coffee. He looked at me for a moment in silence before saying, "It feels different now."

"Yes, it does," I said. "But not in a bad way."

He shook his head. "No. Just… deeper."

That night, we sat by the window and watched the rain slide down the glass. The sounds of Rome came back: the voices from the street and the plates clattering in the café below. He reached over and wiped a drop of rain off my shoulder.

"Do you think fate exists?" he suddenly asked.

"I did before," I said. "Now I believe in choice."

He smiled. "Then maybe choice is just fate that needs courage."

He kissed me slowly and with certainty.

We lay in the dark later that night, with our hands resting on each other. We didn't have to rush or explain what we were. It just was.

For the first time in years, I wasn't afraid of love.

CHAPTER FIFTEEN

Florence

Our apartment in Rome was small, but it was full of life. The morning light came through the lace curtains and softly covered the books and sketches. The smell of coffee and candle wax was in the air. We could hear our neighbours arguing about dinner and then laughing about it again through the thin walls. It all made the place feel warmer and more like home.

We built a rhythm without even realizing it. Near the sofa, Giovanni's favourite books were piled up in uneven towers. As my notebooks spread across the table, they looked like spilled petals. Most mornings, we burned toast. He would squint at the newspaper, pretending to read, and forget his glasses. After I teased him, he would grin, and the day would unfold. Perfection was never our goal. It was presence.

We would walk to Campo de' Fiori on Sundays with a basket that had more holes than sense. We bought figs, basil, tomatoes, and bread that broke when you tore it open. Giovanni said hello to each vendor by name. Everyone loved him. Even the grumpiest seller calmed down when he spoke. People thought he was like the person they wanted to be.

We found a café between two flower shops where an old man played the accordion and his wife served tiramisu that made you close your eyes right away. When the world was too loud, we would go there. We would sit in silence sometimes, just listening to the sounds of life around us. That café reminded us that happiness doesn't have to be big. It can live quietly, like a normal day.

The city got softer at night. The streets were bright. Giovanni would read aloud from his favourite poets, like Neruda, Rilke, and Calvino. His voice made even tired words come alive. I would sit next to him with my journal, and the sound of his voice would match the scratch of my pen. He looked at me over the candlelight and said, "This is happiness."

I said, "It feels like home."

We lived in Rome for almost two years. I stopped counting from the office or the divorce. I was counting from the first time I walked into Libri e Caffè in the morning. The city taught us to wait. It taught us to live in the present instead of chasing after it. Even though we loved it, we could feel a quiet restlessness growing between us, as if something were waiting just beyond what we knew. We would drive to Amalfi on the weekends. The road there twisted and turned like a ribbon through lemon groves and cliffs. We stayed in a small villa that belonged to a cousin. The air smelled like salt, and laughter seemed to last longer. Those days were great, but I think we both knew that things were going to change.

Florence started to yell at Giovanni. At first, it was just a passing thought, but then it became a pull we couldn't ignore. He said, "It's smaller. More human. A city that breathes with its art." At first, I didn't want to. I had a rhythm and roots now. But the more he talked, the more I felt it, too. Rome had changed us, but maybe Florence would make us even more so.

We sold some things and started to make plans. Moving isn't a romantic thing to do. It's counting coins and turning off the power. It's sitting on the floor with boxes, wondering if you are brave or stupid. Giovanni sold a box of collectible journals that he had kept since he was in his twenties. "Everyone owns stories," he said when I complained. I realized that love is often more practical than poetic.

We left on a cool spring morning. The train north took us past olive fields and small towns that looked like prayers that had been forgotten. I put my forehead against the glass and watched the countryside change. I felt both loss and a new beginning. The whole time, Giovanni held my hand. We didn't say much. Words can't describe some changes.

Florence welcomed us with light and stone. It was cooler there, and the air smelled like the river and dust. We found a small apartment on the Oltrarno side that was only two rooms wide and not very deep. The floors creaked and the shutters wouldn't open, but we could see the Arno blush pink every night from our balcony.

We took our time building our home. A table that had been used before. Two cups with chips. We hemmed the curtains ourselves, and they were crooked but cute. Everything in that small space had a heartbeat. The smell of coffee and the sound of church bells woke me up in the morning. Giovanni got a job helping out at a friend's bookstore. I wrote at the window that looked out over the narrow street where kids were chasing each other, and the smell of fresh bread came up from the bakery below.

The bookstore became a part of him. He was meant to be around books, not just sell them but bring them to life. He spoke to customers as if each one were a story that needed to be read. Some days, he came home with fewer books than he had when he left because he had given them away. I made fun of him, but he just smiled and said, "Stories are meant to travel."

Like linen on a clothesline, our days caught light and wind. We worked, cooked, fought, and made up. Love wasn't in big gestures, but in little, unseen ones. For example, he would leave the light on for me when I worked late, and I always kept an extra spoon for his coffee because he lost his.

Giovanni called our old Fiat our "little miracle," and one afternoon we drove it out into the country. The car shook like loose change, and the radio only played one station, but it was ours. A tire went flat somewhere close to San Gimignano. Giovanni said he could fix it. He laughed, then coughed into his sleeve and waved away my frown. He said, "Dust. This is what the roads are made of." I thought he was funny because he was so sure of himself. An hour later, we were both covered in grease and sitting on the side of the road, eating apricots that a nice farmer had brought us. The sun was low, and the fields were gold and green. For a moment, it seemed like the whole world was humming in quiet approval.

That night, Giovanni turned to me and said, "You know, I think this is it."

"This?" I asked.

"Home. Not the right place. This. You and I, the way we keep finding joy in the cracks."

I nodded. "Then let's never stop looking for it."

Florence showed us how to fit in with each other and with a place. We learned how to walk in the streets. We got used to the smell of the river, the way the bridges curved, and the sound of laughter bouncing off the walls in narrow alleys. I bought tulips on market days and put them in a glass jar in the kitchen. We took the train to Pisa or Lucca on the weekends and ate slow meals in small trattorias, talking about nothing and everything.

Giovanni asked, "Do you think this will ever get old?" one evening as the sun set over the Arno.

I said, "Never. With you, every day feels new."

He smiled and moved a piece of hair out of my face. He said, "You've changed. You walk like you know how valuable you are."

I said, "You taught me how to love."

"And you taught me to believe in it," he said.

We were quiet as the river showed our faces and the light changed from gold to blue. At that time, I thought that if life stopped, it would be enough. But life doesn't usually stop at perfect times.

I noticed the cough around that time. It started out small, like something that would go away. Giovanni didn't care. "It's the dust from the road," he said with a laugh. I wanted to trust him. Yes, I did. He still had the same fire in his eyes and warmth in his touch. But at night, when the city was quiet, I could hear him breathing heavily and feel something cold move through me.

One night, I saw him sitting by the window with a cup of tea that he hadn't touched. The lamp's light made the lines around his eyes look darker. "Are you all right?" I asked.

He smiled, but it was a tired smile. "Just a cough, Sophia. A little wine can fix anything."

I tried to laugh, but it got stuck in my throat. The moment was over. That night, we didn't talk about it again.

Life went on, even though things were starting to get a little shaky. We walked to the water. We read. We made love. We acted like we didn't see what was happening. Because love isn't always about not being afraid. It's about keeping it quiet and choosing happiness anyway.

We were still young enough to think that time would keep its word. We thought we had more days, more sunsets, and more breakfasts that made us laugh. We might have. Maybe we didn't realize how fragile time is until it starts to bend.

As I lay next to him and listened to the sound of his breathing, I thought about all the little things that had brought us here: the burnt toast, the street markets, the laughter, the soft arguments, the late-night readings, and the apricots by the side of the road. Every piece had been a string. They had built a life together.

He rolled over in his sleep and grabbed my hand, wrapping his fingers around mine. I closed my eyes and whispered a quiet prayer to the dark: that this life we had built, which was both normal and extraordinary, would last a little longer.

The cough was still there the next morning.

And the next morning after that.

We didn't know what was going to happen yet. The light still made the floor look gold. The coffee was still steaming between us. That day, love was all that mattered.

The Shadow and the Light

Giovanni's cough didn't go away. It stayed with us through the morning, the quiet hours of writing, and the evenings when the city was settling down. At first, it was light, like nothing at all, but it got darker quickly. Giovanni tried to laugh it off and said that the dust from the books was to blame. He said he needed stronger coffee, not a doctor. I wanted to believe him, and for a while I did.

Weeks turned into days. He got tired more quickly. He was out of breath after climbing the stairs. At night, I would wake up to the sound of him coughing into the pillow, which he would do to keep me from hearing it. But I always did.

The curtains let in soft, golden light one morning. He sat at the table with his hands around a mug that he hadn't yet picked up. His eyes met mine, calm but impossible to read.

He said softly, "I think I should see someone."

It wasn't fear in his voice. It was acceptance.

The doctor told them to get tests. The volunteer table at the hospital smelled like antiseptic and lilies. Giovanni made everyone laugh by joking with the nurse and asking her about her favourite books. That was him. He always put others' needs before his own, even when he was scared.

The doctor spoke slowly when the results came back, as if each word meant something. I heard words like "malignant," "lungs," and "treatment," but they didn't make sense. Giovanni sat still and nodded, as if he had been expecting it. I looked at him, expecting him to deny it or get angry, but he just took my hand and said, "We will take it one day at a time."

The smell of rain was in the air outside. For one crazy second, I wanted to throw the folder into the river, tear up the pages, and give them back to the sky. I squeezed the cardboard so hard that my fingers hurt. I almost pulled my hand away and let the anger speak first. Instead, I swallowed it and let it burn all the way through my chest. He gently squeezed my hand, which helped me feel more grounded.

He whispered, "No drama. We live the days we have. That's all we can do."

I nodded, but inside I was screaming.

In the first few months, there were a lot of hospital visits, medications, and long afternoons that all seemed to blend together. He got thinner. The ring slipped off his wedding band finger because it got so thin. One afternoon, we took it off together and threaded it onto a small cord. He laughed and said, "Now it's closer to my heart." I felt both the joke and the pain at the same time. But there was still light in his eyes. We read together while we waited. We talked about normal things like music, recipes, and the next trip we would take when he got better. Hope wasn't a dream; it was a way of life.

I would sometimes see him standing at the window and looking out at the river. "What are you thinking? Please tell me," I said.

He smiled a little. "That I'm lucky. Not everyone gets to love like we did."

One night, he asked me to get him a glass of wine. The doctor said no, but I did it anyway. He sipped it slowly, with his eyes half-closed. He said, "It still tastes like summer. Do you remember Amalfi? The lemons, the sea, and the light?"

I nodded and swallowed the pain in my throat.

He said, "I thought that would be the best time of my life. But it wasn't. It is now. Here, with you. At this very moment."

We didn't talk after that. The quiet was enough.

Over time, I learned a new language that was made up of small gestures and quiet care. The way I held his arm while we walked. When he breathed hard, he leaned into me. The way we could laugh even when we were in pain. When I put him to bed one night, he said, "You were always the braver one."

I shook my head. "No, Giovanni. I'm just following your lead."

He chuckled softly and then coughed. "My light is getting dimmer."

"I'll keep it alive," I said.

His sickness turned into a love map. Every time I went to the doctor, every night I couldn't sleep, and every time I held on became a prayer. Our world had shrunk to the space between breaths, the warmth of a hand, and the sound of a heartbeat next to mine. The world outside kept going.

There were days that were good. Days when he was strong enough to walk by the river again, when he stopped to buy tulips for the table, and when he hummed old songs to himself. Those days felt like time borrowed from someone else, a gift that didn't cost anything. And there were bad days when pain took away his voice, and I had to learn to speak for both of us.

During those months, I wrote again, but my words were different. They were slower and easier. I wrote about how brave little things can be. About what it means to stay. People who read my work wrote back. They said that what I said helped them get better. They didn't know I was writing to save my life.

The sky over Florence turned grey one afternoon. The rain started out softly and then got louder. Giovanni was sitting by the window with a blanket over his shoulders and looking at the river.

He said, "I used to think healing meant getting better."

"And now?"

"Now I think it means loving the time that is left."

I moved closer and put my head on his shoulder. His skin was warm, and his breathing was shallow but steady. "Do you ever wish things were different?"

He said, "No… Yes, I wish I had more time. But not in a different way. You and I—this was enough."

We stayed like that for a long time, with the rain running down the glass and the sound of it mixing with the sound of his breathing. There was nothing else that needed fixing. Just to feel.

The night he got worse, the city was quiet. I sat next to him, held his hand, and counted each breath. He opened his eyes and said softly, "Promise me something."

"Anything."

"Keep on living. Continue writing. Let what we taught you help you stay open."

My vision was blurry from tears. "I don't know how to live without you."

He smiled, but it was weak and slow. "You already do. Since the day we met, you have."

His hand relaxed in mine. His breath became slower. And then, it came to a stop.

I couldn't move for a long time. I couldn't get any air. My mind wouldn't accept what my body already knew. Then the questions came, all at once, crazy, childish, and holy.

Why him?

Why this man whose kindness kept whole rooms together?

Why did he love so gently, ask for so little, and be patient with the world when it didn't give him any?

Why not someone else?

Why not anyone else?

Why tell this story? Why now?

I wanted to make a deal with the air so that I could wake up in a different version of my life where he was still there, complaining about burnt toast and touching my shoulder like it was the most normal thing in the world. I wanted to scream his name until the universe admitted it was wrong.

For a short, horrible time, I hated every quiet morning he ever gave me because I knew there would be no more.

The room suddenly felt too small, too bright, and too cruel to hold the truth in the middle of it.

Grief is a harsh and strange teacher. It doesn't come politely or leave room for reason. It takes your breath away and leaves you standing in a world you don't know anymore. It comes in waves that don't make sense and pulls you under even when the sun is shining. No one tells you that grief can feel like fear, anger, or numbness that scares you more than pain ever could. No one tells you that grief is a slow process, that it requires effort, and that it changes every morning.

But sitting there next to him, I learned the truth: being sad is not a sign of weakness.

It is how love won't go away.

I whispered, "Come back," and put my forehead on our hands.

But the room stayed quiet.

Grief doesn't care about reason. It rips through you like a storm, leaving nothing where you used to be sure. I sat there asking questions that didn't have answers because that was the only way to stay awake.

Much later, the silence got softer, and I could stand up.

The silence that came after was heavy but not mean. It was like the world was holding its breath in memory of what had happened.

For hours, maybe longer, I stayed there tracing the lines of his face and memorizing them one last time. When the body dies, love does not die. It gets into the air.

The morning light came through the window and softly fell over him, just like it did the first morning we woke up together. I said "thank you" in a whisper because I had no other words.

I walked to the river later, when the city started to wake up. The pale sky made the Arno shine. I stood on the bridge with the wind in my hair and felt him all around me: in the sound of the water, the smell of coffee coming from the cafés, and the way my heart kept beating.

I didn't feel empty. I felt full, sore, and alive.

I wrote this that night:

Love is not what we lose. It is what we bring with us.

And for the first time in a long time, the page didn't scare me.

CHAPTER SEVENTEEN

The Legacy of Love

The days that followed didn't seem like days. The air was flat. The rooms were still warm, but it was a warmth I couldn't reach. I walked through it like it was a picture.

The last page he read in his book was open. I walked away from it. His scarf hung over the chair he always sat in. I also left that. There was a faint ring around a coffee cup on the counter. I told myself I was busy. The truth was easier. I was making little altars.

I went back to Rome with no plan, just pain. I rented a room with a balcony that got the light from the evening sun and made the roofs look gold. I sat there and heard a city I loved sound different. I still heard him. *Take a breath, Sophia. Take it easy. Look up.* It didn't fix anything. It helped me keep my breath.

Grief didn't move in lines. It came in waves that I couldn't plan for. Whether I was standing on Roman cobblestones or a dusty road in Lagos, sorrow knew every street. That sound had shaped the earliest parts of me, long before Rome ever softened my edges. It follows you like a second spine that won't bend. I lost Giovanni, and it broke my heart. It also made me stop speaking a language I had just learned.

It was a dull stone under my ribs some mornings. It knocked me to my knees for hours. A laugh on the street that sounded like his. A scent. The way he said my name—*Sofia*, with the weight on the second syllable—made me feel like someone was behind me. Comfort and pain at the same time.

I walked on old paths. The streets had changed. A gelato shop window where we used to fight playfully. He would smile and say, "Of course, it's dinner." Two scoops is a full meal. Three is a party. I cried and smiled at the same time. I kept going.

I sat on a cold bench in Piazza Navona one night. Kids ran around tourists in a zigzag pattern. By the fountain, a violinist played something I had never heard before. For the first time in weeks, I didn't feel like I was being torn apart by other people's lives. I let the sound wrap around me. Gratitude crept in next to the pain. *Thanks for letting me know him. Thank you for love like that.*

He was everywhere. A man leaning on a railing, not in a hurry. A woman pointing out the moon to her friend. Two people looking at each other as if the square has disappeared. He would have stopped, pointed up, and said, "Look." Sometimes, the moon doesn't follow the rules.

I thought about the first rain, the bell over the door, and the stranger who talked to me about *Jane Eyre*. That was the key. We didn't feel the door turn until later.

His words stayed with me like music does after it's over. He once said, "Life is not about avoiding pain" after we saw a couple fight and then hold on to each other, like they might float away. "It is about carrying it and letting it shape you without making you small." I nodded like I understood at the time. Now those words sounded like they were telling me how to breathe.

He never made me hurry. He never pushed me when I didn't trust the ground. When I pretended to be fine, he put his scarf around my shoulders. He stopped to look at the sky like it was his job. He believed in pistachios like some people believe in hymns. He taught me that little things are enough.

He was no longer there. I wasn't empty. I had his steadiness inside me. I heard, "Take the kind path" when I had to choose. When doubt hissed, I heard, "You are stronger than the story that hurt you." I heard, "Don't go away now" when I wanted to. Love never goes away. It moves to different rooms.

The square changed colour from gold to blue. The violin kept going. I shut my eyes and heard him again. Don't kill yourself to keep your heart safe. That isn't life.

I stood up and put my hand in my pocket. I felt the folded postcard from Tuscany that I had never sent. I opened it and read the simple lines in the dark. It wasn't grand. It was like praying.

I stopped at the edge of the square and looked back. I almost heard him, calm and funny. "Okay. Gelato is dinner."

I told him and the night, "Two scoops."

I saw a store window full of cheap pens and blank notebooks on my way home. I went inside and got one. Not a ceremony. A decision. I sat on the floor at home, opened the book to the first page, and wrote, "I am still here." The old list from my kitchen table came back to me: books, travel, service, and words. I had checked each line without even realizing it. There wasn't a list in the next part. It was a life. After that, I kept going. The square at night. The chair has a scarf on it. The cup is on the counter. How grief changes a city, and gratitude finds a place next to it. I wrote until my hand hurt and the room got dark. I heard him again at our table. "What you say matters."

I walked to the river the next morning. The light on the water looked like a warning and a promise. It didn't feel like the future was a cliff for the first time. There is no big plan. The next thing to do is right. Coffee. A walk. A call I had been putting off. Maybe a train when I was ready. He was crazy about trains. He used to say that leaving the house is the first step to a good trip.

I rested against the rail of the bridge. The city moved around me, both kind and uncaring. I put my hand on my chest and felt it thud.

I told the wind, "I don't know how to do this without you."

The answer came from somewhere behind me, like a favourite song. "The same way you did with me. One thing that is true at a time."

I washed the cup on the counter when I got home. While the water was running, I cried. It still hurt after I dried it and put it away. Something settled underneath it. Not comfort. Not the end. A little truth. You can carry this and stay alive.

That night, I sat by the window and watched the city light up. I thought of him in all the places we had been happy. On top of buildings. In stores. He knelt down on a cobblestone to tie his shoe and called it "ancient sabotage." He would say with a look, "You're safe here."

His love had grown deep. There were more than just things left behind. It was how he taught me to pay attention to what is real. Those weren't souvenirs. They were directions.

What comes next, I don't know. I know there's more. He taught me that chapters can start and end without asking. He also told me that the book keeps going.

I closed my eyes and heard his last words clearly. "Go ahead, Sophia."

I said back, "The world still has so much. I will."

I turned off the lights. It wasn't empty; it was dark. He stayed, like warmth after a fire.

I slept for the first time in a long time.

On the first anniversary, I went to the river with everything I could carry and everything I had to let go of.

CHAPTER EIGHTEEN

The Return of the Sun

I walked to the Tiber with his ashes in a small wooden box on the morning of the anniversary. The city of Rome moved around me in a soft hum, as if it had decided to be nice. Bakers put trays on counters. A cyclist rode through a puddle and kept going. There was a smell of warm bread and exhaust in the air. I kept looking at the river.

The thin sun had already warmed up the stone wall. I could smell wet concrete and coffee coming from a kiosk nearby. The water was brown and steady. I pushed my thumb along the seam of the box until it hurt, and then I opened it.

"Thank you," I said, because words had to be in the air. "For loving me. For teaching me to pay attention to the little things when the big ones hurt. Thanks for staying until I could breathe again."

I turned the box. The ashes fell into the water and started to move. The current took him like time takes everything else, without asking. A little wind blew and brushed my cheek. It felt like a hand. For the first time, I didn't just feel empty. I felt alive. Quiet. Steady. Something inside me let go.

I sat on the wall and watched the river hold what I had given it. I remembered how he always laughed a half-second after he smiled. I thought about how he would have said, "Look at the light on the water" if he had been here. "See how it keeps going?" I stood up and walked when my legs started to shake.

I didn't hurry. I let the city come to me in bits and pieces. A florist taking the ties off of the buckets. A boy pulling his mother toward a pastry case.

A woman with a red scarf was talking on the phone and nodding as if the voice could see her. I walked past Sant'Andrea della Valle and went inside. The air was cool and smelled like stone and candles. I sat in the back and let the deep blue of the dome calm my breath. I didn't pray with words. I let my body do the praying.

The light got sharper outside. I went to Campo de' Fiori and bought pears that I didn't need. The seller wrapped them up in paper and didn't ask me for anything. I carried them like it was a ritual. The fountains at Piazza Navona spoke their own language. I stood where we used to fight over gelato. He would say that it should count as dinner. I could hear it so well that I had to close my eyes.

I was tired by late afternoon, the kind of tired that comes from being sad, like every thought was as heavy as a stone. I took the long way to Libri e Caffè and stood outside the window. The bell above the door still made that soft sound. Isabella wiped down the counter and looked up. Her eyes got softer. She didn't ask how I was doing. She came over, hugged me, and said, "I made lemon biscotti." I nodded because lemon helps you remember how to taste.

We were sitting at a table next to the shelves. She pushed the plate toward me and poured espresso. I told her about the river. She listened while her hands were still on the saucer. She filled my cup again when I ran out of words and didn't try to break the silence. When I stood up to leave, she put a small, wrapped package in my bag.

She said, "For later. When the quiet gets sharp."

As the sky turned the colour of a peach left on a windowsill, I walked back to the apartment. I made pasta with garlic and oil and used more salt than I usually do. I ate at the counter in the dark. The window showed the city moving like a slow tide. I washed the plate after dinner, dried my hands on his old towel, and pressed the fabric to my face until I could stand up again.

I opened the window in the bedroom to let in the cool night air. The dresser had an empty box on it. I didn't put it away. I lay on the bed and watched the ceiling change from grey to black. I could see the ash letting go when I closed my eyes. I heard his voice, low and close, like it sometimes does in dreams.

"Take a deep breath, Sophia. Look up."

Grief stayed. It learned how to sit without taking every chair. Hope started to grow in the space next to it. I didn't have a plan. I had mornings, and that would have to be enough for now. I wrote three lines before bed.

I took you to the water.

The city took me back.

We both kept going.

I got up early the next morning and walked to the market again. I bought tulips that were the colour of a light bruise and put them by the window. I did little things all day long, as if they could teach my hands how to live. I folded towels. I put books in order. I made a soup that tasted like love. When night fell, I thought about the Amalfi balcony and how the sea changed from gold to rose to violet. Like warm water, calm came over me.

I said "thank you" to the horizon that I couldn't see but could still feel. "For how to live. For how to love. For how to have hope."

The stars came out when the sun went down. It didn't feel like an end. It felt like my breath was coming back.

I had been putting off opening the drawer, but when I finally did, I found his handwriting waiting for me: a single envelope with my name written in his careful script, brought up with the rest of the mail by the concierge.

CHAPTER NINETEEN

A Letter to the Future

The apartment was quiet, except for the soft hum of the city below. Rome sounded different now. It was quieter, as if the cars knew how to speak more softly. Time had done little to smooth the edges after thirteen months.

The rooms still had the shapes of us in them. His scarf hung over the back of the chair he loved. He'd left his glasses on the counter, where he would never reach for them again. His books were lined up patiently with their spines facing out and underlined in a way I knew better than my own.

I stood at the door to our bedroom with a small box and a promise to be brave for as long as it took. I carefully put his things in straight lines on the bed. Pens that he liked. Ferry tickets from Positano. A folded receipt with a note in the margin that says, *Don't forget to show Sophia the page about the bridges.* I touched the ink with one finger, hoping that warmth would come through it.

I saw it then.

The drawer I had been avoiding for months was half open. I pulled it all the way. Shirts that were folded. A watch that was broken and needed to be fixed. An envelope was under them. My name was on the front. His handwriting was bold and careful.

It made me stop. My throat got tight. For a long time, I just held it, tracing the S's curve and the pen's slow pressure. I remembered how he tilted his head when he wrote, how he hummed to himself softly, and how he would stop in the middle of a sentence to smile at something he hadn't said.

I finally broke the seal. The paper smelled like soap, old paper, and him. I sat on the bed's edge and started to read.

My dearest Sophia,

If you are reading this, I am no longer here. I can only guess how heavy this moment is. I wish I could hug you, kiss your forehead, and tell you to take a deep breath. This letter is my way of hugging you since I can't.

You gave me a life that I didn't know I needed. You were the light in my days and the sound that kept my mind steady. When you first walked into the café, wet from the rain and asking about Jane Eyre, *I knew that something in me would never be the same. I remember thinking that your face might be what courage looks like.*

You made our rooms smell like toast and basil, sound like pages turning, and fill them with laughter. You made the normal things holy. You made me think that love could be quiet and still feel like it would never end.

You said, "This feels like home," when we sat by the Arno last summer. You were right. You were my home.

I hope you'll understand why I had to leave. I tried to stay. I fought against what I couldn't change. But life can still be full, even when it gets shorter. You made mine full.

Please promise me that you will keep living. Not just getting through the days for the sake of it. Live with the same sense of wonder that you brought to every café, market, and book you read. Go back to travel. Write again. Laugh loudly in places where the sound echoes. Find your heart again.

Don't see this as the end. Love never ends. It just moves to a different room. You can find me in the warmth of your skin, the wind that blows on your cheek, and the way the light comes through the kitchen window.

Don't turn away if someone comes into your life and looks at you the way I used to. I want you to fall in love again. I want you to feel the world around you open up. You deserve it.

Every sunrise you think you're watching alone; I'll be there with you. You are never alone.

Always yours,

Giovanni

The words got blurry. I held the paper to my chest and cried until the sound filled the room. I ran my fingers over the page again when my breathing got back to normal. The ink had faded a little where my tears fell, but it felt like he was sitting next to me at the table.

I looked around the room. The space that was empty didn't feel so empty. His scarf, his books, and even the dust on the shelves were no longer old things. They were proof that something beautiful had happened and had meaning.

It started to rain outside, and it was light and steady. I went to the window and saw it draw soft lines on the glass. The lights of the city behind them flickered and turned golden.

"I can't do this without you," I said into the silence.

The silence didn't say anything. It held the truth like a palm holds water.

When my tears stopped, I folded the letter and put it on the nightstand next to his last book, which was still open to the page he had never finished. I touched the edge of the paper and said, "I'll try."

I kept his words in my pocket for days after. I read them on benches in the park, on buses, and in the corners of cafés. They helped me calm down. Live. Let my heart open. Let the world in. Every line felt like a little bridge back to me.

I took the train to Florence one morning. I told myself it was work, but it was really an escape. Or maybe come back. The rain came next, soft and steady. I found a small café with a window seat at the station and ordered a cappuccino. I put Virginia Woolf next to the cup. The heat rose into the cool air, making little ghosts that disappeared too quickly.

The bell above the door rang politely. A man came in and shook the rain off his coat. Dark hair with silver streaks in it. Eyes that were calm and took in the room without needing to own it. He gave an order and then looked at my table.

"Is this seat taken?" he asked.

I said, "No." It sounded like my voice had remembered how to be soft.

He was sitting across from me. We let the rain speak for us for a while. Then he looked at the book.

"Virginia Woolf," he said. "A good friend on a rainy night."

"You read her?"

He grinned. "*To the Lighthouse*." The room that every woman should have. Sadness. And the stubborn act of making it happen anyway.

We talked. About art. About cities that both hold you and let you go. He told me his name was Daniel and that he restored frescoes for a living, bringing stories back to life. When he talked, his hands moved and made shapes in the air.

We walked when the rain stopped. The cobblestones sparkled and looked like little fires holding pieces of the streetlights. He walked me to my door and stopped.

"Thanks," he said.

"Why?"

"For the business."

I smiled. "Thanks, too."

We stood in the calm that follows rain. He leaned in and kissed me once, slowly and carefully, as if he were asking me to let him live.

It didn't feel like being betrayed. It felt like air. It felt like I was walking into a room I had only seen through glass before.

That night, I opened Giovanni's letter again. *Let your heart open.*

I kissed his signature and said, "I'm trying."

The room was quiet, but I could feel something moving in it. Not a ghost. A fresh start.

CHAPTER TWENTY

The Interval Between

The days after meeting Daniel went by like warm air coming in through an open window. Nothing was in a hurry. Nothing was asked for. Every morning when I woke up, the city seemed possible again. I could make coffee and not break while the kettle sang. I could write with a pen on paper at my desk without feeling like the page was a wall.

We didn't make plans that scared us about the future. He sent a short text in the afternoon. *Are you able to go for a walk?* I replied, *I can meet you by the bridge at six.* We kept our word for an hour, and then we let things happen as they would.

He took me to the flea market by the river on Sundays. He knew where the stalls were that had old pictures in cigar boxes. He gave me a stack, and I fell into the lives of people I didn't know. A woman with a scarf tied around her neck was leaning into the wind on a pier. Two girls with ice cream cones in their hands and their heads tilted toward the sun. A couple with their knees touching and their eyes closed, sitting on the steps of a church. We were quiet as we looked, and then we traded what we had found.

He was kind with his curiosity. He wanted to know about the bookstore in Rome, where I first went in the rain and met a man who gave me a cappuccino and a place to sit. He didn't push for the parts of the story that were still fresh. When I gave them to him, he caught them and put them down gently.

He let me see his world. A brush, a ladder, and a tray with shallow cups of paint. Under a high apse, we stood together while dust floated in a shaft of light like slow snow. He dipped his brush and then lifted it to a dark piece.

At first, the green looked like a stain. It got brighter and took the shape of a leaf under his hand. He worked in silence for a long time, and I watched his breathing slow down as he focused.

He said, "A lot of this is just patience" without looking down. "You look until the story comes out."

He moved out of the way so I could see the small part he had finished. A vine wrapped around a post. Two hundred years ago, someone had painted it with care. It had been hiding in smoke and time. It had been waiting for hands like his.

I said, "You bring things back."

He smiled and washed his brush. "Only what wants to come back."

After that, we walked along the river without rushing. Families walked by with paper cones full of roasted chestnuts. A dog pulled on its leash and then lay down with its head on its owner's shoe. The air smelled like wet stone and sugar. I told him about Amalfi and the cave where the water made the walls look like green glass. I said that the light looked like it was breathing. He listened while he walked. Completely. It was as if what I said was a piece of a bigger picture that he couldn't see yet.

When we crossed the street, he reached for my hand. I was surprised. Not the touch itself but the fact that my body didn't move. His hand was warm. His grip didn't claim. We held on while we walked to the station, but when we got to the steps, we let go without saying a word. That's how it was back then. Nothing was stolen. Everything was available.

Evenings with him took place in small rooms. There were clean walls in the gallery with black and white photos on them. A kitchen with two stools and a bowl of ripe pears on the table. A café with a window that acted like a lens for the rain. He would sit up straight and pay attention easily. He was calm, like someone who had learned to wait without making noise.

We talked about normal things at first. What is a good tomato? What street has the best light in the late afternoon? Then the conversation got deeper in a way that wasn't obvious. We went from talking about food to books to loss and then back to food, as if they all lived in the same house.

The letter was in my drawer at home. Some nights, I opened it up and ran my finger over the signature. *Let your heart open. Let the world in.* It was like being led through a dark room by a voice I trusted. I would close my eyes and hear him laugh like he couldn't help it. After that, I would breathe. There were some nights when I didn't cry. At first, it felt like betrayal. It felt like rest later.

There were times when guilt came up without me asking for it. I reached for a bunch of basil at the store and thought of Giovanni's hand brushing mine in the kitchen, where we burned toast and laughed about it. I had to leave my basket on the counter and go outside to get some air. The street moved around me like I was in water. I leaned against a wall and let the feeling go. I put my hand over my heart and talked to the pain in a voice I hoped was kind. You can love both the past and the present. Breathing does not mean you are breaking a promise.

Later, when Daniel and I were sitting on my balcony with cheap wine in chipped glasses, I told him about it. Someone's open window let the wind carry rosemary and salt.

"I held fear like a shield for so long," I said. "Being happy sometimes scares me because it feels like forgetting."

He nodded his head. "I get it," he said. "Happiness is not being rude. It can be thanks in action."

He didn't try to change my mind. He never made me happy by arguing with me. He made a place where happiness could sit down without worrying about whether it belonged.

The first time he stayed the night was like most nights. We made a simple meal. Oil from olives. Garlic. Anchovies that melted in the heat and left behind only a strong salt. He told a story about a wall in a small chapel outside Siena where the paint had come off in petals, and he had to figure out how to put them back on one at a time. I told him about Mateo, the man who learned to read when he was older and said "thank you" like it was a piece of glass he had polished himself.

He took our plates to the sink and ran water over them in a steady line after we ate. There was a lot of talk and steam in the room. He dried his hands and stood still after doing the dishes, as if he were listening for something. He looked at me with care, as if he were asking something.

I walked toward him. He got closer to me. He kissed me slowly. The kind that asks and waits. I answered with my mouth and then with my hands on his shoulders. I could feel my body waking up. Not because of hunger that makes you feel full but because of welcome.

We walked through the rooms with the lights turned down. He ran his fingers over my wrist like he was reading a line of poetry. I held his face and felt how soft the skin is at the temple, where hair turns grey first. It felt like leaving the door open to a room where the night could move without knocking when we took off our clothes. We were not afraid, and we were careful. The bed welcomed us. Time slipped away from us.

I have been loved in a way that was too strong. That kind of fire leaves behind ash where a person used to be. This wasn't that. This was warmth that went all the way to the bones. He said my name in a soft voice, as if it were a word that could bless. I said his name and felt my throat open and relax. We didn't hurry to the edge. We let the tide come and go until it felt like we had found a safe place together.

He then put his forehead against mine and shut his eyes. We took turns breathing. He fell asleep with his mouth on my shoulder and his hand on my hip. I watched him for a long time and didn't feel like he was watching me. The room wasn't empty; it was dark. I thought about the letter again. *Please promise me you'll keep living.* I said it back to the ceiling. "I'm trying."

We didn't act like we were already a story with a title in the morning. He would go early when he had to. He would put on his coat, kiss me on the forehead, and leave a note if I was still asleep. *Thanks for last night. Talk to you on Tuesday.* He didn't write a lot of declarations on the page. He let the days talk for him.

He made me laugh without even trying. He couldn't peel an orange in one long strip. He said he would be able to do it by June, but he always failed. He took a wrong turn on streets he had known for years, but he didn't care. He said, "This is how you find your new favourite doorway." He opened a gate for an old man on a bicycle and bowed like a waiter in a fancy hotel.

The old man laughed, shook his head, and kept going. Daniel felt good about making a stranger smile.

There were also hard times. We were two people who had built lives that didn't expect each other. He had a regular schedule for his days that didn't include my storms. I had storms. They came in the mornings when the light hit the empty chair just right. I found one of Giovanni's long black hairs curled behind a bottle in the shower. It had been there by accident for more than a year. They came in the spring when the city smelled like the Amalfi Coast. He would notice if I stopped talking.

He would ask, "Where are you?"

I would say, "With him."

He did not leave the room at that time. He didn't pull me back with force. He sat down next to me and rubbed the small of my back in slow circles with one hand until I could breathe again. We didn't act like I hadn't left when I came back.

"I don't need you to fix anything," I told him once when the sky was getting dark and the air outside smelled like rain.

"I know," he said. "I just want you to know that I'm here when you look up."

Some nights, we walked to the river and stood on the bridge where people lean over to talk or be quiet. He put his forearms on the stone and stared at the water while I stared at him.

"Do you ever feel like you're failing the past by making a new present?" I asked.

He didn't answer right away. He looked at the current move and the light on it. He said, "I think the past wants us to grow. That's how it stays alive without crushing."

He told me about a painter who had painted the same wall three times over the course of three decades. Each layer covered a different time in his life. Fight. Getting married. A late happiness. Each layer broke and let the other colours show through. Daniel said it wasn't his job to pick which life to honour. His job was to make sure they all stayed alive.

That's how it started to feel for us. No replacements were made. Nothing was deleted. The layers stayed. The new colour came through, but the old colours stayed true. My chest felt bigger. There was space.

I began to write more. Not just letters to the man I'd lost. Not just entries that sounded like prayers. I wrote about things that happened at the market. A boy stealing olives one at a time while his mother traded for citrus. A woman holding her bread close to her heart like a baby. A cat that thought the bookshop was his and sat on the reference shelf with a look that said, "Don't even think about it." I wrote about frescoes and how colour can sleep for a long time and then wake up when a brush touches it. I wrote about touch that doesn't take and love that doesn't crowd. I wasn't worried about what would happen to any of it. The pages stacked up like folded clothes. Clean. Waiting to be used.

We took the train to a small town on a Tuesday in early spring because the ticket was cheap and the weather looked good. We climbed a hill where the grass had yellow flowers on it that looked like confetti. He lay on his back and stared up at the sky. I lay next to him and watched as his shirt moved up and down with his breath. He looked at me, and his eyes crinkled. Then he reached for my hand. It seemed like the easiest thing in the world.

"I don't know what this is," I said. When I heard the words, they surprised me. They didn't scare me.

"I don't either," he said. "We don't need to know yet."

I thought about how many times I had tried to name things so I wouldn't feel lost. This was something that needed to be left alone for a while. I let that go.

He fell asleep in the grass, and I watched him. I felt peace come over me like a small, brave animal. I didn't feel like my heart was still covered in gauze for the first time since the hospital. I still missed Giovanni so much that it made me feel weak. Some nights, I woke up with tears already on my face. When the wind got too close to my bones, I still wore his scarf. But still. I could hold two truths without breaking them. Love was still there. It had changed shape and told me to grow with it.

A week later, I asked Daniel to join me at the little shop near the piazza for the book circle. Isabella had started it with me so that people could sit at a table when they didn't know where to sit. Daniel sat in the back with a small bag of biscotti tied with a string. He heard a woman read a page about how she lost her mother. He rubbed his eyes with the heel of his hand like someone does when they don't want to be seen. He put the biscuits on the table and said, "For courage." The woman laughed and cried at the same time.

He walked me home that night, and we stood in the hallway outside my door. The light wasn't very good. I could feel the cold floor through my shoes. He looked like a painting in a museum. A man standing at a door with something he didn't want to drop.

He said, "I'm not here to take anyone's place. I'm only here if you want me to be."

"I do," I said. For once, my voice sounded clear.

He leaned in to give me a kiss. It was nice and simple. He put his hand on my cheek, and we stood there for a long time, just because it felt good to be close.

The days kept getting longer. They sometimes opened like flowers and other times like knots. I began to feel a different kind of tired. It was the kind that wouldn't let you sleep and wrapped itself around your bones. I had to open the window and breathe in fresh air some mornings because the smell of coffee made me sick. I told myself it was the time of year. I told myself that the work was going too fast. I told myself stories and let them sit in the room without checking them.

I took the letter out again on a quiet night. The paper had gotten soft because I had folded it too many times. I read the lines that told me to open my heart and let the world in. When I put it down, the wind from the open window lifted the corner like a tiny hand. I stayed still and listened.

Some truths don't come all at once. They gather.

A period that didn't happen. A sleep that covered whole afternoons.

A sudden softness in a body that had been trying to harden for years.

The idea came to me like a soft knock. It didn't push. It stayed still.

I put my hand on my stomach and felt nothing and everything.

The room stayed the same. I changed inside of it.

A quiet understanding spread through me like tea darkens water.

I didn't say the thought out loud. Not yet.

I stood by the window and watched the evening move across the rooftops.

The city changed colour from gold to blue in one long breath.

I let that breath flow through me.

The phone rang on the table. Daniel. "Are you awake? I'd like to bring some oranges."

I smiled. "Yes. Come."

He came with a paper bag and the smell of cold air in his coat.

We took the peels off the oranges, but they didn't stay whole. We laughed.

I closed the door and leaned against it after he left.

The apartment heard. The city changed.

I put my hand on my stomach again and felt a soft certainty that didn't need proof.

Life was creating a small space inside of me.

I still didn't know what that meant.

I only knew that the time between sadness and happiness had gotten longer and was now full of something new.

I went to the window and opened it more.

The curtains moved as air moved through them.

I said "thank you" with my eyes closed.

Not to anyone in particular. To the time to get there. To my heart for not closing when it had every reason to.

The river would keep flowing all night long. Tomorrow would ask its questions. For now, it was enough to stand in my house with the letter open on the table and a sweet taste in my mouth. The beginning of something quiet was taking its place in the dark.

CHAPTER TWENTY-ONE

The Turning Light

It took a long time for the morning to come, as if the day itself wasn't sure it was coming.

The sea below seemed like it was half-sleeping, with slow, steady breathing. The light flowed across the surface in tentative, unsure strokes, like someone who was learning how to paint again. I sat on the terrace with a cup of coffee that had long since gone cold. The air smelled like rosemary, salt, and a little piece of the past.

Daniel had already left before the sun came up. He had carefully scribbled a note on the counter that said:

Thanks for believing in me. See you soon.

I grinned when I read it. The words were straightforward and easy to comprehend. Honest person.

The house was silent, but for the first time in years, the quiet didn't make me feel sad. It felt like a cozy room inside my ribcage. The heaviness in my chest had changed; the sharpness that mourning used to have had morphed into something gentler that I could embrace without getting hurt.

The days that came after moved like sunlight across a wall: slowly, steadily, and without any noise. Daniel went back to work on fixing things. I returned to my pages. We saw each other when we could, and when we couldn't, we lived as if we were breathing in the same rhythm.

In the morning, he would email me a picture of the sky. I would send him a sentence that I was having difficulties with. That was all.

Laughter came back into my life without asking for permission. It was not the loud, room-filling laughter of escape but a gentle chuckle of endurance, the kind that arises after overcoming a situation that could have broken you. We took too long to eat. It was simple for us to walk in solitude. When our hearts needed a break, we gave them one.

And something began to shift below all that warmth.

It started off as a whisper. A fatigue that I couldn't name.

Mornings when food tasted like metal in my mouth. Scents that were too strong for the air. I thought it was the time of year. Work. That old, persistent sadness that was in my bones.

But one afternoon, while I was on the balcony reading Giovanni's letter, the truth hit me that I had been returning to his words for comfort, not because they were changing but because I was.

The wind picked up one corner of the page, as if it wanted to breathe too. Light quietly blessed the ink. And my hand moved to my stomach without me meaning to.

A little motion. But everything around it stopped: the water, the air, and even my own heart.

Is it possible?

It wasn't a loud discovery. Like daybreak, it was a creeping, wobbly clarity that came over me.

One hand on my chest. One hand on the smooth curve of my belly. And below that, a faint, magnificent heartbeat.

I thought about the times Daniel and I had spent here at night. Not the passionate, blazing love of fiction but the calmness of being seen without having to do anything. The ease that comes when two people are no longer striving to be more than they are. Life had come in through that quiet safety, like a guest who wasn't invited but somehow fit in.

The doctor said I was forty-nine years old and pregnant, and the statistics didn't matter. The only thing that mattered was the strong, steady heartbeat. The kid would come when I was fifty.

Someone from back home once told me, "The harmattan haze cannot forever hide the sun." There is always a way for light to pass through.

Hope felt like that now: quiet and patient, not loud or sure.

My mom used to say that when something new starts to grow inside you, like a dream, a faith, or a kid, the world gradually becomes quiet so you can hear it. I finally realized it when I stood there and cried.

And I remembered what Giovanni had told me:

"Life will surprise you when you least expect it."

There was no betrayal here. This was a continuation. This was a change.

His love hadn't gone away; it had only shifted direction.

I said "thank you" in a quiet voice to the air. Maybe to Giovanni. Maybe to Daniel. Perhaps it could be attributed to the life within me. It didn't matter. There was a sense of gratitude in everything.

As the last light faded over the sea, I put Giovanni's note back on the desk. I didn't fold it up. I gave it some time to breathe and recover.

I stood near the window as the church bells rang below. I could still hear him say, "Promise me you'll keep living."

"Yes," I answered quietly.

The first light of day warmed my palms. I didn't know what would happen next, but for the first time in years, I wasn't terrified to find out.

The sea was black and buzzing outside, and it was late at night. The talk suddenly turned to names. Daniel suggested gentle Italian ones. Pretty and melodious. But none of them stayed with me.

He touched my knee lightly.

He inquired, "What did your mother call you when she was at her best? Before things got busy."

My mother came back to me right away. I thought of her in the small kitchen in Lagos, flour on her hands, her voice turned toward memory. She would tell me stories about the village where she was born, the red earth and the tall trees, evenings when the sky felt close enough to touch. Once, she told me about a name she loved as a girl. Nebechukwu. She said it slowly, letting every syllable rest on her tongue. Not as a command, she said, but as an invitation. When the road is rough, lift your eyes. There is always more than what you see.

Sitting there with Daniel, one hand on my belly, I heard her voice again as plainly as the waves.

I said "Nebechukwu" out loud.

He repeated it again, this time with care. "What does it mean?"

"Look up to God," I said. "Look up when the way feels closed. My mother used to say the sky is the one road that never ends."

Daniel smiled, but it was a sweet smile that was unusual.

"Then it's perfect," he remarked in a quiet voice. "She is already a promise to keep looking up."

The name settled over the room like a benediction. It made me think of my mother's town, the red earth of my infancy, the Lagos evenings that made me who I am, Giovanni's insistence on light, and Daniel's steadfast hope.

I tried the short form. "Nebe." It felt right. At the same time strong and weak.

A bird called twice from outside.

Even though we had chosen her name together, I hadn't informed Daniel of the truth that was steadily growing inside me: the life itself. Coming up with the name was simple. The confession needed a little more courage.

I would tell him tomorrow.

Tomorrow, the world would alter again.

Open Roads, Open Hearts

This morning, the sea is calm. It hears.

The waves move slowly, folding into each other as if they have nothing to prove. Light rests softly on the water, soft gold floating over blue. I sit on the same balcony where I first kissed Daniel, thinking of the river where I scattered Giovanni's ashes and where I learned that grief and grace can live in the same breath. My daughter, Nebe, is six years old now. She's in the next room, stirring and asking her first impossible question of the day. I'm fifty-six now, and the woman I was in Rome feels like a long-lost relative whom I love.

Life softly echoes in the next room.

I put my hands on the railing and shut my eyes. There are still mornings when the pain comes back out of nowhere, like when I smell coffee, hear a train in the distance, or see an empty chair that still seems to be waiting for someone who will never come. But it doesn't break me anymore. It sits quietly next to me now, softened by time and love.

Daniel is on the steps below, drawing in his sketchbook. He draws slowly, like someone who thinks with their hands. He smiles and looks up sometimes. We don't talk at all sometimes. The silence between us has changed. It is no longer heavy. It is full.

Giovanni still shows up in my dreams some nights. He stands by the window of our old apartment, hands in his pockets and a small smile on his face, as if he always knew I would keep going. When I wake up, I cry, but it doesn't hurt. It feels like something nice is coming to see you.

The paper in his letter has gotten softer over time and is now in a box next to my bed. Sometimes, when Nebe moves, I read it out loud to this small, lively heartbeat. I tell it that there was once a man who loved with quiet certainty and taught me to see the world differently. We named her Nebechukwu, which means 'Look up to God' in Igbo, my mother's language from her village. My mom said it to me for the first time in our kitchen in Lagos with flour on her hands. She said that when the road seems closed, you lift your eyes. "The sky is the only road that never ends," she said. Daniel and I picked it out together because it has all of that. The red earth where my mother was born, the city where I grew up, the men who taught me to keep my heart open, and the promise that there is always light above the haze. Most of the time, we call her Nebe, but when I want her to remember that love never ends, I say her full name. It changes its form. It learns how to talk again by using new names.

I go to the little bookstore near the piazza most days. The shelves are a little crooked. A record player that crackles more than it plays old jazz. I teach a writing group on Thursdays. We sit around a long wooden table with half-empty mugs of tea and talk about the truth, not how perfect things are. I say what Giovanni told me again: Stories don't have to be perfect; they just have to be true.

Daniel sometimes comes close to closing time with paint on his fingers from fixing up an old wall. He stands in the doorway until I finish reading a sentence out loud. We then walk home through the narrow streets, stopping every now and then to stand by the river. There is nothing to say.

The ordinary is now peaceful. The market smells like lemons. The way books feel under my arm. The six-year-old's steady beat as I fall asleep.

Some nights I write letters that I never send. To Giovanni. To Nebe. To the woman I used to be. There are no big statements; only small truths written in soft light.

Thanks for staying as long as you did.

Thanks for letting go when you needed to.

Thanks for coming back in a quieter way.

I put the letters on the desk and leave them there. You don't have to read every word. Some people just need a place to sleep.

The house smells like warm bread tonight. Daniel puts away his sketchbook and hums to himself. I stand by the window and watch the sea turn dark blue. Nebe moves, as if to remind me to breathe.

Love feels bigger now. It holds Giovanni, whose laughter I can still hear in my head. It has Daniel, who built something strong and patient next to me. It holds this child, a quiet promise that life will keep going.

And deep down, I feel another rhythm beneath it all. A pulse like the sound of traffic in the distance on a Lagos night. Restless, alive, and reminding me of where I started and how far I've come.

The sky gets brighter. The sun rises and shines gold on everything it touches.

I take a breath that feels like a new start.

I whisper, "Thank you."

For the pain that made room for love.

For the love that showed me how to have faith.

For the hope that turned into a life of its own.

I close my eyes and feel the light on my skin.

I am not the woman who hid from her grief.

I am not the woman who forgot how to breathe.

I am the woman who learned how to live again.

And maybe love isn't about holding on forever.

It might be about keeping your hands open and trusting the ground beneath your feet.

The world opens, and I open with it.

"On Places, Healing, and the Roads That Shape Us"

This book was never just about places.

It was about what places make us feel.

Rome. Florence. Amalfi. Tuscany. Lagos. I didn't write these cities down as places on a map. I wrote them down as states of mind. Each one stands for a season inside: rediscovery, rest, awakening, surrender, and renewal.

I haven't walked every street in this book with my feet, but I have walked them with my heart. I found some of these places through research, books, movies, documentaries, travel journals, Google Earth, and hours of quiet watching. I looked at their light, their rhythm, and their silence. But more importantly, I heard what they meant to people who had gone there looking for something.

I wasn't trying to write down geography.

I was trying to follow the path of a heart that was learning how to live again.

Sophia's journey is not just a story of love and loss. It is the story of someone who had to stop talking to stay alive but then slowly started talking again. It's about a woman who lost her voice and then, word by word, city by city, breath by breath, found her way back to herself.

The story is made up, but some of the things in it are true. I know what it's like to start over. I know what it's like to leave home in search of something that isn't fully defined. I know what it's like to carry the memory of Lagos traffic like a heartbeat, to miss the harmattan winds that sting and comfort at the same time, to build quietly while others guess, and to live through seasons where survival feels louder than dreams.

Like many people who leave home, Sophia carries belonging as both a comfort and a pain. Even when she is far away, Lagos lives in her heart. Florence calms her down like a quiet evening in Jos. The rush of Amalfi's light makes me feel like I'm at Erin-Ijesha Waterfalls, small, humbled, and yet whole.

Sophia isn't tied to one country or one identity. She is a lot of us: immigrants, dreamers, healers, wanderers, people who have loved and lost, people who have gone quiet and dared to speak up again.

This book isn't a romance in the usual sense. It talks about how love changes us even when it doesn't last. The death of Giovanni is not meant to hurt the reader. It is meant to remind us that some people come into our lives to wake us up to something we were too scared to touch. Daniel's presence is not a replacement; it is a quiet sign that the heart can open again without forgetting the past. The child is not a surprise. It is hope that makes life.

I wrote this story for people who have:

- loved deeply and lost quietly
- walked through grief that had no name
- rebuilt in silence while the rest of the world tried to guess
- had wounds they didn't choose
- began again when they weren't ready
- been scared that their story was over
- got brave in a quiet room
- found healing not in big miracles, but in small, steady breaths

Thank you for going down this road with Sophia.

Thanks for hearing the silence between the words.

I hope that something in this story makes you feel like you are not alone in your journey, no matter where you are reading it.

May your own paths open up.

May your heart find space to start over.

And may you always remember that journeys are still journeys, even when they are quiet.

Thank You,

Rufina Ajalie

About the Author

Rufina Ajalie is a storyteller whose writings are rooted in emotional truth, exploring the tender terrain of loss, courage, becoming, and the miracles of starting over.

For nearly two decades, her professional career as an HR and People Strategy leader has lived at the intersection of humanity, change, and resilience. She has helped organizations reimagine how they lead, grow, and care for their people, grounded in her core belief that:

"People are the soul that makes strategy come alive."

This deep understanding of transformation, healing, and the many ways humans break and rebuild themselves shapes the emotional landscapes of her writing.

Born in Nigeria and now joyfully rooted in Saint John, NB. Rufina's personal migration story echoes the movement, hope, and second chances found in her debut novel, Open Roads, Open Hearts.

Her life and work continue to champion inclusion, courage, and the beautiful, stubborn resilience of the human spirit.